"Are you a cowbo... -4198

He stiffened. The... him the wrong way and he wasn't sure why. Being labeled as a "cowboy" reminded him of the ranch. Of his dad. Of everything he didn't want to be. He was different from his old man—*he* rode rodeo. *He* was going to be a winner. She didn't know he was a Hartmann. It was better when they didn't know.

"I am," he admitted, digging deep to brush back the wave of caution. It had been a long time since he'd kissed a redheaded stranger.

She wasn't exactly a stranger. She was Hannah, the devil on his shoulder reminded him. She bit her lip. Perfect teeth. Was it weird that he noticed that?

"Then I guess it doesn't matter." She smiled. "Because I *never, ever* kiss cowboys, friends or not."

* * *

How to Catch a Cowboy by Katie Frey
is part of the Hartmann Heirs series.

Dear Reader,

I love reading about tortured heroes and heroines, not to mention a love story with a twist. When I learned about the opportunity to write a series set in Montana, I spent a *lot* of time researching (and not *just* shirtless cowboy pictures). I became fascinated with the concept of breaking and training horses, more specifically, taming the part of an animal that is wild. This brought me to my characters, each wild and independent in their own right.

Hannah and Jackson are both smart, fierce, independent... and a little wild. We typically see alpha males with beta females, but in this story, I was excited to write two alpha characters who find that, in love, they *both* have a soft side.

I loved every moment spent writing and editing Jackson and Hannah's love story. This is a story about family. About belonging. About finding the part of you that is maybe the most difficult to love, and finding someone who understands it. This is a story about grief. About passion. About wanting someone else's happiness more than you want your own.

I can't wait for you to read it.

Bisous from the Alps,

Katie

Please say hi: Instagram @romanceinthealps, Goodreads/BookBub: Katie_Frey or, more embarrassingly, TikTok @romanceinthealps.

KATIE FREY

——

HOW TO CATCH A COWBOY

ISBN-13: 978-1-335-58157-0

How to Catch a Cowboy

Copyright © 2022 by Kaitlin Muddiman Frey

For questions and comments about the quality of this book,
please contact us at CustomerService@Harlequin.com.

Harlequin Enterprises ULC
22 Adelaide St. West, 41st Floor
Toronto, Ontario M5H 4E3, Canada
www.Harlequin.com

Printed in U.S.A.

Katie Frey has spent the better part of her adult life in pursuit of her own happily-ever-after. Said pursuit involved international travel and a few red herrings before she moved from Canada to Switzerland to marry her own mountain man.

A member of a tight-knit critique group and avid writer, *How to Catch a Cowboy* is her second novel for Harlequin Desire. She wrote the bulk of the book in a local coffee shop... Any excuse to stay near the fresh croissants!

You can join her newsletter here: bit.ly/3COLHoP

For her author website: www.romanceinthealps.com

Books by Katie Frey

Harlequin Desire

Montana Legacy
How to Catch a Cowboy

Visit her Author Profile page at Harlequin.com, or romanceinthealps.com, for more titles.

You can also find Katie Frey on Facebook, along with other Harlequin Desire authors, at Facebook.com/harlequindesireauthors!

This book is dedicated to Jennifer Catalano, who listened to me prattle on about these characters more than I ever dreamed a friend could, would or should.

One

The Hurt

"When you're an athlete challenging an angry opponent ten times your weight, odds are you're gonna get hurt. And you're probably gonna get hurt bad." The words stuck in his throat, but Jackson Hartmann didn't know what else to say.

What else *could* you say to someone who had had the stuffing kicked out of them by an 800-pound bull? Offering comfort had never been a strong suit for Jackson, which he supposed shouldn't surprise anyone given he'd been essentially raised by wolves. Not that his present company had any idea of his wolf pack heritage.

"That's real sweet of you to say." Mikey, his mentee, twirled his hat on a pointed finger before indulging in a deep drag of pale ale. "Course, you gotta admit the odds tend to look better on you these days." Mikey frowned at him, and Jackson felt a rise of embarrassment heat his face.

Jackson's victory tonight had been swift and well earned. He'd stayed on Viper, the meanest bull this side of the Yellowstone, three seconds longer than the next best cowboy. Mikey hadn't made it five seconds before being thrown across the arena.

"Yeah, well, I've taken my falls the same as the rest of you." Jackson leaned his weight forward, resting his elbows on the varnished bar top. This place was a far cry from the staffed kitchens of his youth, not to mention the polished accoutrements so prevalent in his family's privileged lifestyle, but he was a man on a mission. Perhaps the contrast with his own upbringing was half the allure of the rodeo circuit. That, and there weren't any Hartmanns in this neck of the woods.

Country music blared through tinny speakers and cigarette smoke hung low in the room, absorbing the reflection of neon lights. The no-smoking sign? Apparently more of a suggestion than a rule. This was Montana and, following a rodeo, there were a different set of rules for the cowboys.

"Hey, circuit champion!" Will, the youngest in their group, bumped against him, grooving to the banjo beats that filled the room. The blonde buckle bunny on his arm pressed her body into his side, hanging on his every word.

"What's the bet tonight, boss?" Mikey quipped. He swept the peanut shells littering the high-top table onto the floor, crunching them under a steel-toed boot.

"Haven't had enough losing for one evening?" Jackson dished, an elbow digging into his friend.

The bets had started as a way to distract themselves from aches and pains. Bets like who could kiss the first blonde, then who could take home a girl with a belly button ring. But none of it had aged well and the tradition now held no appeal for Jackson. He was, however, a crushing minority in that respect.

"Don't you think you're getting a little old for these games?"

His rebuke went unnoticed.

It had been hard enough for him to fit in, having grown up as the youngest son of the largest landholder in Montana. That's where the pseudonym came in.

"You always were a class act, Brad," Mikey answered, rubbing his stomach ruefully.

Jackson gave the practiced smile he now adopted as second nature. His alias, Brad Hill, was an armor, protecting him from the real hurt. A hurt way worse than anything that could happen to him in the arena. Maybe that was why he was so good at rodeo riding. He *liked* getting hurt. Especially when it was a hurt he chose. Sort of.

Brad Hill was the name on his original fake ID. The first chance to drive a stake into his share of the Hartmann legacy and put some much-needed distance between him and his father. Now, with the Professional Rodeo Cowboys Association championship on the horizon, a chance to make the name he'd chosen for himself was more important than ever. And the name he'd make famous? It wouldn't be the one he'd garnered from dear old dad.

When asked, he'd offered the pseudonym by reflex, just shy of a decade ago when, as a runaway, he'd met Rodney "HotRod" McAllister. No looking back since. He'd now answered to Brad for so long, he wondered if on some level it wasn't his real name.

Jackson nodded toward the bartender, a blonde inundated with drink requests. The flood of orders didn't sway her. He slapped a ten on the table, waving away her offer of change. She'd earned it, and the last thing that motivated Jackson was a few bucks.

He supposed the boys were right to be jealous. It had been a big win tonight. A gold-buckle win and the purse to go with it. Of course, by the time HotRod took his cut, Jackson would be left with substantially less. That was their deal. At least, for now. Truth was, it didn't matter much. Money only mattered to people who didn't have any.

Tonight he was going to let the boys have their fun. In the meantime, he'd drink.

"Don't you think it's a little disgusting?" The voice insulting him was anything but. His ears perked up to an adorable Boston accent, chewing on the words and sounding delightfully foreign in this neck of the woods.

He shifted on his stool, spinning to address the mystery woman. He swallowed, suddenly dry-mouthed despite a generous sip of Scotch only moments earlier.

She was beautiful. Unconventional perhaps, but undeniably beautiful, red hair with strawberry highlights tucked behind dainty ears. "I beg your pardon, ma'am?"

"Ma'am? Now you break out the chivalry? Might be more effective if I hadn't heard you discussing bets about women only moments ago."

She was making fun of him. Her reproach wasn't serious; at least, he didn't figure it was. Large blue eyes sparkled at him, as though daring him to deny it. *Too bad this one isn't wearing apricot.*

"As it happens, I'm particularly fond of women."

The bartender placed a fresh drink in front of the woman, who smiled appreciatively. *So she does have a soft side.* As she reached into her purse Jackson waved her away, putting another ten on the countertop and offering, "Please, this one's on me."

Jackson watched as she picked out the straw, licked an errant drop of the minty drink from the tip and put it on the countertop.

"Straws are for children." She shrugged, as though totally unaware of the way his body tightened in response.

"I'm Brad." He extended a hand, hoping she'd take it.

"I'm Hannah." She smiled at him. "Thanks for the drink."

Hannah. She must be new to the circuit. He hadn't seen her around, and she stuck out. A fish out of water, no denying it. True, she wore the standard uniform of blue jeans and a plaid shirt, but her shirt was oversized, looking more like a man's shirt than a fitted top. She'd tied in a knot just above the waist of her jeans. She was curvy. Soft. Delectable. And precisely molded to his taste. Hannah wasn't wearing a cowboy hat, but that megawatt smile? This wasn't just another girl chasing the rodeo. Hannah was *all woman*. It was hard not to appreciate her.

"That's quite a smile," he noted aloud. His observations served mainly to improve upon what he had falsely assumed was perfection.

"I've had a great day," she admitted, taking a sip of her drink while keeping eye contact.

"How's that?" It was difficult, not being drawn in by her smile.

A moment of shyness passed over her and she lifted her glass so quickly some of the drink spilled over the edge. Her eyes searched for a paper towel dispenser or cocktail napkin. Finding none, she lifted her glass and licked again, up the side of the cup. Then she caught his gaze and darkened to the same shade as her hair. "I had an interview today. A job I really wanted. It went better than I'd hoped."

In an effort to look anywhere but at her knotted shirt, he stared at her drink. "Oh yeah, what's that?"

Her blush was starting to fade and Jackson studied her face intently. She had a light sprinkle of freckles across the bridge of her nose.

"It's not the job, so much as the opportunity. No one thought I could do it. Or that I should *want* to do it." Her chin jutted forward as though he had been a part of the offending "no one." He swallowed, reckoning this little ball of fire could do pretty much anything she damn well set her mind to.

"So what's a nice girl like you—"

"Doing in a place like this?" She laughed. "Obviously giving in to a lapse in judgment, accepting drinks from strangers." She smiled again. Her good mood was infectious.

"Hey, I'm not a stranger, I'm Brad. Your new friend, Brad."

"Ahhhh, so we're friends now?" She looked him square-on, eyes widening under her raised brows.

"Sure." He gave a slight shrug, fighting the niggling feeling of regret at having been friend zoned with such efficacy. He was losing his touch.

She leaned forward. "Well, that's too bad."

Her whisper, warm breath smelling like bourbon and mint, hit him at the base of his neck. It was hot for July, the sticky kind of hot that made everything seem more sinful than it was.

"Too bad is it? Why is that?" In what he had hoped was a subtle move, he inched his stool closer to hers.

She just may be what the doctor ordered.

"I don't tend to kiss my friends."

Or not.

"See, I think you're closing the door on a world of opportunity." It was amazing, his ability to speak through the thick wave of disappointment. It shouldn't matter. The last thing he needed to do tonight was to kiss a stranger. Then again, she wasn't a stranger, she was *Hannah*.

"That so?"

Was he hallucinating, or had she dragged her stool a little closer to his?

"It might be."

"Are you a cowboy?" The words dripped from her.

He stiffened. The question, while innocent, rubbed him the wrong way and he wasn't sure why. Being labeled as a cowboy reminded him of the ranch. Of his dad. Of everything he didn't want to be. He was different than his old man; he rode rodeo. *He* was going to be a winner. She didn't know he was a Hartmann.

It was better…better when they didn't know. Still, it would be nice if, for once, it wasn't about *what* he was but *who* he was.

Brad Hill.

Geez, he was going soft. Viper must've hit harder than he realized.

"I am," he admitted, digging deep to brush back the wave of caution. It had been a long time since he'd kissed a redheaded stranger.

She bit her lip. Perfect teeth. Was it weird that he noticed that?

"Then I guess it doesn't matter." She smiled. "Because I *never ever* kiss cowboys, friends or not."

Hannah turned her attention back to her drink and Jackson exhaled a hot breath. *Never kisses cowboys? This is Montana. Who else is she gonna kiss?*

Not me.

Redheads were trouble anyway. Whatever.

"So that's it then?"

She was talking to him again.

"Well, if you don't want to be friends…" He smiled at her again despite himself.

"I didn't say I didn't want to be friends, although I don't know you, apart from your offhand comments about women." She grinned. "I just advised that I don't kiss my friends."

"Or cowboys," he clarified with a grin.

"Specially not cowboys." She tilted the rest of her drink down, maintaining a static gaze in the process.

"Excuse me." A new woman pressed against him, holding his gaze a minute too long. But she was too obvious. He looked past her, focusing on Hannah. She was frowning, obviously unhappy her new friend was the recipient of additional female attention. So maybe Boston wasn't so cut-and-dried after all. Jackson wasn't the sort to back down from a fight. *If it isn't hard, it isn't worth it.*

"No problem." He dismissed the clumsy blonde and smiled back at Hannah. "I'm not sure what kind of friend I'd be if I didn't at least toast to the success of your mysterious interview."

They don't grow 'em like that in Massachusetts, Hannah considered as she lifted her glass to meet Brad's cheers. "Thanks," she managed to breathe.

In another life, Brad was exactly the kind of cowboy who would mean all sorts of trouble for little old Hannah Bean. And in that past rebellious life, she would've leaned forward, hooked a finger through that belt loop and closed all the space between her and Brad. But she'd left that life behind. Acting out due to an absent father was just a little too textbook, and there was another way to get her father's attention.

Undeniably, it would help if he actually *knew* she was his daughter. But she had a plan. First, get the job, prove to be invaluable, earn his respect, then bam! Tell him, *Rodney, I'm your daughter.*

There was no room in the plan for a man like Brad, delicious though he may be. But he had a point. It was tough celebrating alone.

"Can I ask what brings you here from Boston?" The cowboy, officially the sexiest man she'd ever seen in real life, nodded at her as though he agreed implicitly that whatever reason had brought her to this bar tonight was a good one.

"You can ask." Try as she might, she couldn't stop antagonizing him. Maybe it was because she knew nothing would happen between them. She didn't have to play hard to get, she *was* hard to get—an unfamiliar feeling she quite liked.

"All right. You've got me. I'm asking."

Another insipid woman, half-drunk, bumped into him. "Brad, you were phenomenal today." In a move that lacked all subtlety, the blonde held up a scrap of paper. *My number*, she mouthed, tucking the slip into his front pocket. She pressed her elbows together with a hyperbolic emphasis on her cleavage then winked.

That was one way to go about it, Hannah noted.

"Much obliged." He dismissed her politely.

So, he's a gentleman indeed.

"A plus for subtlety, that one." Hannah swallowed the memory of trying a similar move only a few months ago, hoping she hadn't looked half as desperate in her execution. "Phenomenal were you?" She couldn't help herself. She pushed her elbows together in an exaggerated lean, offering up a brief giggle as she mimicked the blonde's move.

"Everybody's got an opinion." He smirked, fishing the paper out of his pocket and balling it up. "Can we get another round?" He smiled at the bartender and winked at Hannah.

Brad chucked the balled-up paper into his spent glass, sending the unsolicited phone number to swim amid the ice cubes.

"I came for the interview. Here, I mean. Not the bar, I

mean Montana." She surprised herself with the answer. She hadn't been intending on honesty, but watching him brush off the second woman in a row made her feel that he'd somehow earned a little truth from her. The attention was throwing her game, and she was babbling.

"Ah, yes, the elusive interview." He was too close to her, under the guise of needing to lean in to hear her over the bass of the Keith Urban music, but she liked it. So she leaned in, too, in an entirely different way.

"I need to earn a little money. Set aside some savings before I start my residency this fall."

That got his attention. The line of muscle along his jaw tightened and the cleft chin bobbed as he nodded. "Residency? You're a doctor?"

"A resident," she corrected before he could ask again what a girl like her was doing in a place like this. The last thing she wanted was not to fit into her dad's world. She cleared her throat. "Basically, I have my learner's permit for medicine. The pay's pretty bad, though, so I'm here for the summer. I start in September. Bozeman Health."

She wouldn't have seen it had she not been looking. The flicker of dislike that crossed his face. "Something wrong with Bozeman Health?" The drinks arrived, offering a welcome distraction from the interrogation.

"Wrong? No, of course not. I grew up around those parts. Pretty far from Boston, aren't you?" He was steering the conversation away from him. Away from Bozeman. *Odd.*

"Hey, I took the residency that was offered. It's a little competitive in the medical world, in case you haven't heard." Admittedly, that was only half of the truth, but she'd just met the man and wasn't likely to see him again. She didn't need to get deep. Didn't need to tell him that after a decade of searching, she'd found the man her mom had confessed was her real father, and he'd been living in Montana ever since leaving them both. Truth be told, getting any honesty out of her mom was only possible in the brief sober stints between embarrassing drunken episodes. That didn't matter now. She'd looked after her mom her whole life, and now she was close to finding her father. Maybe, just maybe, she'd find someone who wanted to look after her for a change, or at least get to know her. Be proud of her, not just intermittently sober enough to ask for money. Now she had a plan to meet dear old dad. Twenty-eight years of waiting had come to a glorious conclusion and a job offer.

"Thus the interview. For the gig that pays well." Brad nodded again, smiling as he took another deep sip of Scotch.

"Exactly." *Well, kinda.*

The server was back, reaching for her now-empty glass. It was so hot in the bar, she'd sipped it too fast. Or was she just nervous?

"Another round?" Brad asked, pulling another twenty from his wallet. She acquiesced, mostly because she wasn't ready to go home yet.

Maybe the third round was a bad idea. But she was there. In the moment of not wanting the evening to end. Not wanting to stop being the woman who held his attention. She nodded, first to him then to the waitress, and sipped the final dregs of her second mint julep.

In no time, three drinks turned into four and, while

the bar emptied, Brad made no move to leave. Instead he asked her more questions, a heady inquisition she fielded comfortably. The cowboy, on the other hand, offered up very little about himself. The phenomenal display of athleticism referenced by a few other "buckle bunnies," as he'd referred to them, was brushed off in an air of natural nonchalance. He'd won the grand title that evening, that much she'd sorted out.

"Truth is," she admitted aloud, "I don't know much about the rodeo."

"Seems to me, a medical resident could get a way better gig than anything hiring around here."

Better employment opportunities? Sure there were. Truth was truth. She couldn't very well deny it, nor could she admit it. So she did the only thing she could think of to change the subject. Placing her empty glass on the bar top, ice cubes rattling, she leaned toward Brad, looping her arms around his neck and pulling herself up to the tips of her toes. The move got his attention.

"Well, Hannah, what's this? I thought you didn't kiss cowboys?"

"You never asked why."

"The why doesn't matter. You forget, darlin', it's not *my* first rodeo."

She felt his hand drop to her hip, resting there like a sizzling brand of possession.

One distraction. Surely she could handle one distraction without throwing her whole plan awry. Then his second hand met her chin, tilting it up. But, to her great disappointment, he pressed a kiss on her forehead. "Why don't you give me your number, Boston, and we can continue this on the other side of the mint juleps?"

Under crushing disappointment, she blushed. "Yes, okay," she agreed, mostly to avoid dying of embarrassment. If he didn't move his hand from her chin, she feared she'd melt into a puddle right then and there.

If it were possible to want him more, to her consternation, she now did.

He handed her his phone. "Why don't you just make a new contact? Wouldn't want this number to get wet." He grinned, dimples peeking from his stubbled cheeks.

Not his first rodeo indeed.

Two

You Need Therapy

"You did what?" Emily, her best friend, howled into the phone. "How to catch a cowboy indeed!"

"And how's that?" Hannah frowned, not sure she wanted the answer.

"Pretend you're not wildly interested, which I gather you managed to do for *most* of the evening. I can't believe you told him you didn't kiss cowboys. Liar, liar, pants on fire."

Hannah paced the Great Falls motel room, wondering for a moment if the adjoining room could hear the screams through her cell phone. Likely not. The place had been renovated recently, and the roadside motel was now a trendy chic boutique motel. Still, the added insulation didn't calm her mind.

"You know something I don't? I mean I can't remember ever—"

"Tom? That Halloween in college?"

Just like that, she was twenty-two again, making bad
decisions in clubs. "I didn't realize we were rehashing
our most proud moments." She fingered a teak book-
end, wondering if the midcentury-modern touches were
in every room, and how the decorator had managed to
come up with so many vintage finds.

"Just relax, you know I outscore you a kazillion to one
on that front," Emily chided. "What's got you so wound
up? Sounds like day one and you're well on your way to
being employee of the month."

"Hardly." She surveyed the two outfits she had laid
on the motel bed. A white T-shirt was more professional than a black V-neck. She didn't want to be too
overdressed, but fought the fear that she wouldn't be
dressed well enough. Sure, first impressions were important, but second impressions, with her father? They
felt pretty important too. This was her chance to con-
nect with her dad. Impress him, then break the news.

"Daughter of the Year then?" Emily added.

"Yes, that's it, Emily. Hung over my first day, I'm
a poster child for workplace professionalism. Daddy's
gonna be thrilled."

Her stomach rumbled, likely hungry again. Breakfast consisted of jerky, acetaminophen and ginger ale;
hardly the breakfast of champions but thankfully the
painkiller was starting to kick in. The headache was no
doubt punishment for her ridiculous display last night.
She rubbed her temples, willing the spinning behind her

eyes to stop. She had forty-seven minutes before she was due to meet Rod, and she needed to get it together.

"I'm still not sure why you're not working here with me this summer. Boston misses you," Emily said softly. "We've been planning our first summer as 'real doctors' since the first year of med school."

"If we can wait six years to work together, I'm sure we can wait a bit longer. You know I've waited my whole life for this opportunity," Hannah reminded her, pacing the room. She and Emily had been roommates since her first year of medical school and Emily was without a doubt her best friend. Hannah, the merit-based scholarship student, and Emily, the trust-fund student who had proved to be resilient and down-to-earth; they'd made a crack team and hosted the study group everyone wanted to be in. While it hurt to be without her partner in crime, this was something she needed to do on her own. She could hardly lean on a wingwoman to make a good impression with her dad. Plus, if Rodney ended up rejecting her, it might be easier to bear without an audience.

"But, Hannah, you've waited your whole life to be a doctor and now you've taken a job as a massage therapist? And with a rodeo rider?"

"Massage therapy is serious, Em. Rubbing out strains can help these cowboys avoid serious injury, and my background in medicine can make a difference to how I assess and treat injuries in the ER. I mean yes, I'm doing this to meet Rodney, but at the same time, I have an opportunity to participate in a new sector of the rodeo industry. This is a huge opportunity, especially if I ever transition from ER to sports medicine."

"Sports medicine? From the girl who has never even pretended to like any sport?" Emily sounded bitter; she was the sports fanatic in their pairing.

"Well yeah, maybe. If it means working with people I really like." Her thoughts flashed to Brad, and she wondered briefly if he had a therapist. Did winners need tending to?

"Yeah, I bet there are beefcakes galore in rodeo country," Emily howled.

Hannah laughed at the pun then decided on a little salesmanship of her own. "Beats working the night shift changing linens and monitoring the hospice floor."

"All right, all right. You might have a point. I just think this plan is a little crazy. Why wait to tell him?"

"You're right, that's totally less awkward. I should just go up to the man that I have never met and tell him he has a daughter and, surprise, it's me."

"Would that really be so bad?" Emily asked.

"You know, Em, I think the only thing worse than not having a dad growing up, would be to find him now, only for him to reject me. At least, until now, I could explain his absence due to ignorance. How could he be there for me if, simply, he never knew about me? But to find him and have him choose not to be in my life? Yeah, I need him to know me first. To want me. Be clever, Emily."

"You could be a little more tactful. I just don't get the point of throwing away several months working as a masseuse. I feel like this is a recipe for disaster and you know it."

"Your concern is duly noted." Hannah was distracted as she rooted through two small makeup cases in search of her trusty mascara. When in doubt, add mascara. Words to live by.

"At least call me after? I'm in geriatrics this week, trying to remind myself changing bedpans is indeed related to becoming an ER doctor."

"Pretty sure massaging cowboys is better than changing bedpans. Maybe you should ask yourself, Emily, which one of us is making a good choice." She grinned.

"Easy, Tiger, just call me, okay?"

"Yeah. Wish me luck." She whispered the last sentiment to her own reflection, staring herself down in the mirror of her motel bathroom. *Now or never, Hannah.*

The problem with motel beds was that they were too short. Even in these reimagined boutique motels. In fact, it might be even worse in the reimagined boutique motels with their vintage beds. Were people really so much shorter back in the day?

Ten years. It'd been ten years since he left the king-sized beds of his family's sprawling, decadent Montana homestead, and he hadn't been back since. But he had to admit, the too-short beds that came with life on the road were certainly not the selling point for his hard-won freedom.

Austin, his eldest brother, had been the first to leave Bozeman. More importantly, the first to leave Hartmann Ranch following a bitter fight with Nick, Hartmann brother number two. Nick was the good son, committed to building the legacy no one wanted; growing the Hartmann empire. Jackson's move to relinquish his voting shares in the company to Nick had been the right thing to do, the only thing he could do to earn his independence really.

The twins, his stepsisters Mia and Evie, were two years younger than twenty-seven-year-old Jackson, and were the apple of his stepmother's eye.

Josephine wasn't all bad in the world of stepmothers, but she cared a little too much about status. She lived in the manor, a second sprawling property forty minutes away. Offering to cede the deed to Hartmann Ranch and a good part of their inheritance early, had been a power play, and not one Jacks had fallen for; Nick could manage his estate, too, as far as Jacks was concerned. With his father's deathbed insults still echoing in his ears, he knew one thing: he was going to make it without the Hartmann name. And winning the gold buckle of the PRCA championship? The sport his dear old dad had idolized? Earning the celebrity under a *pseudonym* was just the perfect last word to a fight he'd never finish. The last word he'd never get to say.

Jackson was reminded of this on a daily basis as Rodney "HotRod" McAllister's troop migrated from town to town, chasing the circuit, staying in one motel after another. HotRod worked as a rodeo manager, developing Jackson's career as well as Mikey's and Will's. In the early days, Jackson had been happy just to be anonymous, handling the horses and acting as a general yes-man. When he'd first joined HotRod's team, he'd been breaking wild horses, which had felt a lot easier than *being* broken by wild bulls. But the pay hadn't been as good. He wished that didn't matter, but he was six months into a New Year's resolution he couldn't afford to break: rely less on the Hartmann money and prepare to cut the cord with his family indefinitely. It was true. The calls from Nick were increasing in frequency, especially since he'd fallen in love with his new wife, Rose, but Jacks couldn't get attached again. Only people you love could hurt you, and he only liked the hurt he could control. His dad would be the last and only person to hurt him. It was a New Year's resolution for the ages.

Preparing to close the door on the Hartmann wealth was easy. *Had been easy.* But for the first few minutes of every day, with outstretched arms scratched against vinyl headboards and his feet kicked off the edge of the mattress, Jackson allowed himself to admit living in the lap of luxury had had its perks.

A strong sun filtered through the cheap blinds, precisely at an angle serving to interrupt his sleep. Just as well. Reaching for his phone, he was alarmed to see the time: 8:45 a.m. In twenty minutes, he'd be five minutes late for the rundown. He swallowed a burn of disappointment. He half expected she would've texted him. That's what the interested girls did; texted right away or insisted against his chivalry and followed him home. But Hannah? Hannah Bean? She'd entered her contact information into his phone, batted wide eyes at him and bid him good night.

He sank back onto the foam pillow and wondered why he cared. Maybe it was the sloppy attempt at laying one on him, drunk on mint juleps but brazen enough to wrap her arms around his neck. He could hardly have accepted it after she'd insisted that she didn't kiss cowboys. Maybe if she'd had a little less to drink, he would've given in. Lord knows he wanted to.

But no. He slept alone, on the too-short bed. At least

he wasn't hung over. Although it felt a poor substitute for the nirvana he'd have achieved with her.

His mood was not improved by the text that did flash on his home screen. His brother, Nick Hartmann.

Jacks, call me. Livestock commissioner interfering with their broodmares. Can you just come home already?

Classic Nick. Harping once again about when Jacks would be back, the prodigal son returned. Nick was hardly privy to the New Year's resolution. There was time enough to break that news. Jackson stared at the screen only a moment before chucking his phone back on the bed. He wouldn't answer. Sometimes saying nothing was an answer, perhaps the only one Nick had a hope of understanding.

He checked the clock again: 8:47. He could shower and dress quickly and leave himself at least five minutes to indulge in a few more fantasies of Boston aka Hannah Bean.

Yep, he would text her. Jacks never had been one to subscribe to the rules, and there was nothing more ridiculous than the dating game. Yes, he'd just text her. But later, not at eight forty-seven in the morning. There were some rules even he wouldn't break.

"You're late," Rodney McAllister reminded him as he rounded into the diner at five minutes after nine, hair still wet from the shower. Maybe, if he was being honest, he was a *little* hung over.

"Don't see the other men here." He gestured to the

otherwise empty diner. Jackson slid into the booth, tucking his lanky legs under the low tabletop.

"Ordered you a hungry man platter." HotRod smiled. He patted a folded napkin across his temple, wiping away the tiny beads of perspiration that spotted his brow. Rodney wasn't a fool. He might be crooked, but he wasn't a fool. Moreover, he'd been more of a father to Jackson than his own old man, a fact he wasn't likely to forget.

Rodney hadn't changed much over the past ten years. Sure, his skin was a little more lined and his beard had flashes of silver woven through the once reddish-brown hair, but the laugh lines were earned, and the eyes as warm as they had always been. His coach was gruff, but kind, even if his ethics left something to be desired.

"You shouldn't have," Jackson muttered. The diner was stuffy and shabby. One lone ceiling fan issued the only breeze in the room, and the stagnant air was heavy and hot. But at least it smelled like bacon, a redeeming quality for any locale. Jackson cleared his throat. "Look, actually I'm glad it's just the two of us. We gotta talk." An important step toward financial freedom was plugging the holes and controlling the drain. Bottom line? After he won the PRCA championship, he had nothing left to prove.

It was a conversation he'd been dreading, but something was off with Rodney. Jacks had known him long enough to spot it. When Jackson had won the buckle last night, standing amid a roaring crowd, the first thing Rodney had asked was about the purse. Time was, he'd have asked how Jacks was feeling. Jackson had set a personal best on Viper, but he doubted Rodney had even noticed.

But the purse? That had garnered his attention. A few more wins like last night, and Jackson—rather *Brad*—wouldn't need an agent. It was high time he stopped thinking of Rodney as a father figure and saw him for what he really was. A means to an end.

"Me too." Rodney's head bobbled a little too easily, causing Jackson's stomach to turn. The last thing he needed was another person who agreed with everything he said. Just like his stepmother. People who did nothing but tell you what you wanted to hear weren't good for much. They rarely had the backbone to stand up for what was right. He'd take the contrary defiant Boston snark any day.

"We do have to talk. I know that things have been a bit…" Rodney cleared his throat, his chest rumbling as he started coughing. "Truth is, I haven't been feeling my best."

Convenient. Saddling his behavior on an illness.

Nodding at the offered coffee, Jackson smiled his thanks to the matronly waitress. No, he didn't miss being a Hartmann, except the sleeping and eating part. Oh, to be sipping an Italian espresso.

"Know you deserve more, Brad. Truth is, you're the son I never had and I haven't done right by you. But that's all gonna change now."

Sometimes, just acknowledging a problem can solve it. Swallowing the mediocre coffee, Jackson tipped his head in agreement, immediately feeling better about all things Rodney. The son he never had? Did he mean so much to HotRod? Maybe he couldn't be a father figure if he wasn't disappointing. Maybe it was Jackson who was going about this all wrong, saddling the men in his life with expectations that weren't realistic. He gulped. Was he so desperate to find an excuse for HotRod? For his own father?

"It's gonna change, is it?" Jackson lifted his oiled Stetson off his head, slinging it onto the post at the end of their booth. He pushed his hair away from his eyes and dragged a hand along his chin. He hadn't had time to shave and rubbed the scruff thoughtfully.

"Yep. I got a big circuit, twenty-two events in sixty days. I need you in fighting form. We've got to get to the PRCA championships."

Jackson nodded, continuing to rub his jaw, willing himself to unclench. The chance to win at the PRCA championship was paramount to his independence. Paramount to his goal.

Rodney bent, his head dipping level to the table, and pulled the bag up from the floor. From it, he took out a sheaf of papers. From his side of the table, Jackson could see rings of coffee stains and highlighted passages and pen marks, the paperwork heavily annotated.

"What you got there?" His curiosity got the better of him.

"You know I want what's best for you, kid," Rodney said as he shuffled the sheaf of papers into order.

The waitress arrived, placing heaping plates in front of them. Moments later, she returned with the coffee pot, filling their mugs to the top with more of the black liquid masquerading as coffee.

"Before you dig in," Rodney said as he pushed the

papers across the table, "you might want to have a look at this."

It took Jackson a few minutes to register the words on the papers in front of him. *Sponsorship Agreement. Cardic Motors.* Holy hell.

"Is this…?" He swallowed. *No, it can't be.*

"A sponsorship agreement? For the newest, hottest Cardic truck available to man? It is."

HotRod was pleased with himself, as evidenced by the grin spreading across his face, and began shoveling generous forkfuls of syrup-laden pancake into his mouth. The man was rough around the edges but, at the moment, Jackson didn't care.

"Wow." It was all Jackson could manage. Contradictory feelings fought against each other for purchase in his conscience. On the one hand, it was a shot at wealth he could earn himself. On the other? Could he sign a name that wasn't his on a legal document? Were the trappings of wealth just that? A trap? How could he feel both validated and undeserving at the same time? Or maybe he could just sign Jackson and send a copy of his ID? No. If he went to the PRCAs, it needed to be as Brad. Making a name for himself was never the issue. It had to be the right name. A name that had nothing to do with his father. Not to mention he didn't like where this put him with Rodney. A contract naming HotRod as his agent made him one step closer to being beholden to someone else, to having his success tied to another man. No, he didn't like it much. Not at all.

Following Rodney's example, Jackson grabbed a forkful of pancake, digging into the hungry man breakfast before him. But one bite in and his stomach turned.

Yep, he was too hung over for food this early in the morning.

"I knew I could get what you deserved," Rodney said between mouthfuls.

He wasn't agreeing to anything just yet. As far as what he deserved? He was glad Rodney knew what that was, because he sure as hell didn't. His eyes flitted to the spinning ceiling fan, whose fins spun with the concerning wobble.

"I'm not sure this sponsorship is where we want to go. It feels a little bit like selling out." It felt good to voice his concern, even if it was only a half-truth.

"Haven't even gotten to the best part." Rodney's tone imbued the classic flair of salesmanship.

"There's a best part?"

"There are actually quite a few best parts. Along with the Cardic sponsorship, we've got a fancy party, in your honor of course." Rodney smiled.

"Fancy party? Sounds more like a reason *not* to do this," Jackson answered dryly.

"Then there's the truck. They have the new flatbed, all the bells and whistles, for you to drive from circuit to circuit."

Okay, the truck was cool. And it would get him out of the touring trailer.

Rodney leaned forward, sensing his advantage and pressing it. "There's also a cash advance, a hefty one. An interview on cable, a staff massage therapist for the next ten weeks."

"I'm sorry?"

"One of the perks that comes along with the sponsorship is a massage therapist."

"Massage therapist?" Come to think of it, a huge hairy massage therapist might be just what his knotted back needed. This Cardic thing might be worth the hassle, and ten weeks was hardly forever. He and Rodney could part ways a little richer in ten weeks.

Rodney let out a guffaw. "They wanted you. Cardic has been courting you for months. I didn't wanna say anything. You know how these corporate types are, just a bunch of suits."

For a moment, Jackson closed his eyes and pictured Austin, his late brother, suit extraordinaire and the first guy in the room who'd stab you in the back. Hopefully, the Cardic suits had more integrity.

"Eventually, they just asked me what it was going to take to get Brad Hill pushing Cardic Motors at the PRCA championships."

"I wasn't aware you knew what it would take," Jackson said, his voice a little dry. The Cardic gig was interesting, especially signing as Brad Hill. But staying with a mentor he'd outgrown years ago? Less so.

"That's when I asked for a private massage therapist."

Jackson sputtered, sending a shower of coffee over his pancakes. He'd thought Rodney was joking. He hardly wanted a therapist lecturing about his stressed joints, even if at times he was convinced it might make him feel better. "I don't want a private massage therapist."

"You haven't even seen her," HotRod protested.

Her? It didn't matter if it was a woman, he wasn't interested. Jackson pushed back his plate and picked up the sheaf of papers, scanning page one of the sponsorship contract. As loath as he was to admit it, the contract looked pretty good. Better than good.

HotRod broadly waved his coffee cup in the direction of the harried waitress, smacking his lips in the process. "Well, she's coming. Gonna work for the team, a little physical therapy for the boys. I figure she'll be good for morale all around."

"I bet they'll love that," Jackson admitted dryly. A pretty filly was one way to keep everybody's attention, and any bickering about Rodney's commission was sure to be assuaged by a staff masseuse.

The waitress refilled their coffee cups. "I'll take another hungry man platter," Rodney told her. "We're expecting a third diner. Just figuring I'd order her breakfast."

"There's no need for that."

Jackson heard the Boston accent and the hairs on the back of his neck stood at attention. Boston? Here? How small was the world?

"Excellent!" Rodney exclaimed. "She'll order for herself. What would you like, darlin'?"

Jackson willed himself not to turn around. He wouldn't have to, it was a small diner. Sure enough, moments later, he felt her slide in beside him on the bench. Her hip pressed against his; she hadn't so much as looked him in the eye.

"I'll start with coffee." She smiled at the waitress.

Hannah's hair was loose on her shoulders this morning, soft curls reaching halfway down her back. Gone was the oversized men's shirt. Today she was dressed in a fitted T. Once again, he was dry-mouthed. He pushed back the shock of hair that fell in front of his eyes and studied her.

"Brad?" His name was followed by a sharp inhale. What was she doing here?

"Good mornin'," he managed to choke out.

"You've met?" Rodney interrupted the stifled tension.

"Saw her at the bar last night," Jackson admitted.

Hannah colored at the confession.

"Given that you know her, maybe you should be the one to tell her you don't like the idea."

"Don't like the idea?" She turned, squaring her shoulders to his despite the confines of the booth. She was close to him, close enough for him to enjoy a deep whiff of spring flowers.

"I would have pegged you for exactly the sort that needed therapy," she teased. Her thigh pressed against his under the table and Jackson couldn't hold back the grin.

"Is that so?" She might have a point with that one.

"I'd say so. You don't agree? You're gonna send me packing? After toasting to my new position?"

"No, not at all." He ran a hand through his hair and shrugged. "I'm just surprised." That was fair. Surely she couldn't hold that against him. "This was your interview? You shoulda said." The question was more of an afterthought. He scanned the paperwork and folded it in two.

Hannah faced Rodney. "Mr. McAllister, you didn't mention…" She nodded to Jackson.

"Please, call me Rodney," he interjected.

"Rodney…" she tried again, but this time, turning

her full attention to Jackson. "I didn't realize you were the type of cowboy that required the services of a staff masseuse. Is everything okay?"

"Is it?" Rodney directed the question to Jackson.

That's a neat trick. Jackson looked across the table then at the sexpot next to him. Rodney knew him well, well enough to identify and hire an Achilles' heel. A Bostonian redhead with razor-sharp wit and curves in all the right places.

"Yep, contract looks good, HotRod." He shifted in his seat, inching toward Hannah. "Congrats on the job. I look forward to working with you."

Truer words were never spoken.

Three

Chalk It Up to Luck

The coffee tasted like chalk. Hannah sipped anyway, willing her jaw to move, relishing the robotic reflex that helped her to look quasi normal. She forced herself to focus, willing herself not to let her shock break the mask of calm she had practiced on her way to the diner.

She'd set a Google Alert on her dad years ago, the minute her mom had let his name loose. When her mom would binge drink and berate Hannah as a child, she would close her eyes and imagine a future with a father who might want her.

So, when the Google Alert flashed that Rodney McAllister had posted a temporary job offer, it had seemed too good to be true. And when she'd nailed the interview, a celebratory drink had seemed appropriate. But of all the cowboys she could have flirted with, of all the men in that bar, she'd picked the one guy she'd been hired to professionally treat. And what a treat Brad Hill was. True, keeping the shock off her face and avoiding humiliation in the eyes of her father was made all the more difficult by her handsome client.

"You two need to make a plan. I'll need him in fighting form tomorrow night when he rides Beast." Rodney, her unwitting father, was dismissive, issuing the orders without so much as offering up eye contact. It was not exactly the daddy/daughter bonding moment she'd hoped for, but surely she'd be able to impress him with her dedication to the job. That is, if she managed to avoid total humiliation, the odds of which were diminishing by the second. At least she hadn't told anyone about this fiasco, apart from Emily. Not that her mom would have much ground to offer rebuke. She was hardly sober these days.

"I'm feeling fine," Brad said, clearing his throat with a deep "ahem."

"Nonsense, boy. Cardic spends good money to keep you well oiled." Rodney speared a well-cooked sausage with his fork and waved it at Hannah. "After breakfast, I want a treatment plan on my desk. Get it to me before lunch, would ya?"

"Sure. Right away." Relieved to have found her voice, she smiled. Now was not the moment to lose her head, not when she needed it more than ever to impress her father. Rodney avoided eye contact, allowing her the opportunity to work in a knowing nod.

Beside her, Brad relaxed and she felt his muscled

thigh push against hers as he twisted in the booth to face her. "I got a few minutes. Could I walk you to the arena? Show you where we ride tomorrow? Maybe answer any questions you might have about the rodeo?"

That's when she made the mistake of looking at him, sinking into those honey-colored eyes that sparkled at her. The man didn't look one bit hung over. He looked like a Greek god, only better. A Greek god in a cowboy hat. And he was out of bounds. Thing was, her libido had no intention of respecting said boundaries. She flushed. "Sure, um, but I was gonna go to the store. See about, um, topping up on my, er, supplies?"

Maybe it was weak, dodging his invitation, but in the light of day, seated opposite her father, she could hardly give in to the twinge of attraction she'd been fighting all morning. No, she needed to lose herself in denial. She felt the press of a muscled thigh once again touching hers. Yep. It was, without a doubt, time for denial. She didn't want this cowboy. He was a client and a means to an end. And that dimple? Well, it would take more than a dimpled million-dollar smile to throw her off her game.

"I'll bring you. I mean…you're new in town. Wouldn't want some random cowboy giving you the wrong idea. Couldn't want you to make some sort of rash judgment about us rodeo folk because of me."

That's when he did it. The not-so-subtle wink. She felt the electric jab to her gut. *Lord help me. This man is all kinds of trouble.*

"Good. He'll take you." Rodney jabbed his fork in her direction. "Get receipts and we'll expense whatever materials you need." He shoveled the egg into his mouth and reached for his wallet.

"That won't be necessary," she assured him, waving away the twenty-dollar bill he flapped in her face. "I can keep track of everything and send it to you every two weeks. I'm sure I won't need much, maybe just some tinctures and salves."

"I know the perfect place," Brad interrupted. He nudged her out of the booth. "If you're done here, I'll take you, Boston. I can assure you, it's no trouble."

No way out of this one. She swallowed. At the risk of looking the fool in front of her father, she slid out of the booth, wishing for a final time she had put on a little more makeup. She licked her lips then caught the gaze of Brad Hill, who mirrored the action. There ought to be a law against looking that good.

"Okay, I'll get everything I need and—" She shot a sidelong glance to Brad and fought back the blush she felt rising on her cheeks with every ounce of determination that she had. "We," she said as she gestured to Brad and then herself, "will make a plan. I'll have it for you before lunch, Rodney."

"Mmm-hmm." Rodney had moved on to the hash browns and he didn't so much as bother to look up at her. It was okay. She had ten weeks to make an impression. She had waited her whole life for this opportunity. A few more days and she would be in a position to blow him off his feet. The contract was for ten weeks, from now, until the end of the PRCAs. She had ten weeks to get to know Rodney then come clean about who she was. He'd like her by then. He had to. Pushing back her shoulders, she straightened and tried her smile out on Brad, who brightened.

"Right, then, let's go." Sliding out of the booth, Brad issued a dismissive shake of his head at Rodney and walked at a fast clip out of the diner without so much as a backward glance.

He was waiting for her outside the front door. Leaning against the bay window, hips jetting forward, thumbs hooked into the pockets of his jeans, Brad Hill was the picture of masculinity. Too bad he was out of bounds.

When Hannah Bean stepped out into the sunshine, Jackson felt his mouth go dry, despite having drained three mugs of coffee in an effort to combat the final traces of a wicked hangover. She'd looked good last night, from what he remembered this morning. In fact, he'd go so far as to say she'd looked very good. There had been something different about her big-city/awkward country charm, and he'd liked it. Of course now, in the light of day, she looked even better. Too bad she didn't date cowboys. And really too bad that he didn't date *anyone*. With a family history like his, he needed a clean cut to avoid repeating the patterns of infidelity and betrayal his father had set.

Hannah was eyeing him and so he pushed forward, stepping out of the shadow offered by the awning.

"You didn't say your new job was as a masseuse." The words tripped out of his mouth before he could stop them.

"And you didn't say your coach—"

"He's more of a manager," he corrected. She was

jumping right back at him, cutting him off, which he found adorable.

"Manager, then…" She rolled her eyes. "You didn't say your *manager* was hiring one."

"I don't remember you asking." He chuckled then shrugged. "Truth is, I didn't know."

She closed the distance between them and he sucked in another deep breath of floral heaven. Hannah smelled citrus fresh and, for a moment, he wondered how she tasted. Miss Boston was less concerned about her apparent taste and hammered on with her assault of questions.

"Wait. You didn't know Cardic Motors was offering you some kind of enormous sponsorship? You're about two seconds away from rodeo fame…" Her voice trailed off and she blushed, which provoked a smile.

Jackson started walking toward the main stretch of town. He knew how to play this one. Hard to get. Shouldn't be too difficult. He *was* hard to get. Except for a roll in the hay—he was definitely open to that.

Moments later, Boston had settled into pace beside him and, for a quick second, it registered that he was grateful he didn't need to keep eye contact. It was tough to keep his head in the game with such a beautiful masseuse challenging his dating modus operandi. "That would be a great thing—if I was looking for rodeo fame."

"Isn't that the point? Aren't all rodeo cowboys looking for rodeo fame?" Hannah asked.

It was hot, and Jackson adjusted his hat, grateful for the shade the wide-brimmed Stetson offered. "Not me," he admitted. Had it not been for the hangover, he might've put more energy into wondering why it felt important to defend his truth, or even to admit his truth. But it was out now. That was the thing about confessions; they were very difficult to take back.

The high-heeled cowboy boots clicked beside him, offering a rhythmic baseline to his thoughts. It was true, rodeo fame was the last thing he wanted. The last thing he needed. But she had a point. With Cardic Motors behind him, there was every chance he'd achieve the notoriety he'd so achingly avoided.

"Can I ask why that is?"

"You can. I won't stop you."

"Well, if I ask, will you tell me?"

He stopped. Mercifully, they'd arrived at the pharmacy. "Maybe we can get your shopping out of the way first?"

In lieu of an answer, she opened the door and led the way into the old-time drugstore. Jackson stayed by the entrance and watched her as she scanned the shelves and made her way to the back wall. Waving away his offer of help, she immediately began rooting through boxes of tea, of all things. What was she up to?

Mercifully, his phone vibrated in his pocket. He forced his eyes back to the caller ID then decided perhaps fate wasn't as merciful as he'd hoped.

"Don't you have other friends to call?" He was gruff with his greeting, but his brother should know better than to call. Nick was a nice guy, but Hartmann Ranch was the last thing Jackson wanted to be thinking about first thing in the morning, especially in the company of such an attractive masseuse.

"Didn't know we were friends, but I'm certainly delighted to hear you think so." Nick chuckled.

"You always were the clever one." Jackson laughed despite himself. "So what has you checking in so early?"

"I need a reason to call?"

"Don't you?" Jackson's mind was only half focused on his brother. At the other end of the store, Hannah was chatting with the pharmacist, who had arrived with a few glass bottles she'd squealed upon seeing.

"All right, you got me. I'm a man on a mission," Nick admitted.

"A mission, eh?"

"Rose thought maybe you might come home for a long weekend."

Against all odds, Jackson managed to withhold the scoff that followed most family invitations. He liked Nick's wife almost as much as he didn't like going home. Almost.

"Nope, don't think that's in the cards."

"I'm guessing there's nothing I can do to change your mind?" The lilt in his voice betrayed the trace of hope his brother harbored and, for a brief moment, Jackson felt guilty at having to veto it. But his family was just like the women in his life. If he didn't give them any hope, then he wasn't the bad guy for never showing up. For Jackson, not being the bad guy was way more important than he cared to explain.

Hartmann Ranch was the legacy his father was most proud of and, despite the death of Bart Hartmann ten years prior, Jackson couldn't bear to face the ranch his dad had deemed more important than his own sons. No, he'd never go home. If home was where the heart was, then his heart would bleed in the arena, feed on pain and punishment, and maybe, just maybe, the glory of a title he'd earn on his own merit. On his own name. Because making a new legacy that had nothing to do with his father was the only way forward. It was more important than going home.

Across the pharmacy, he heard the chiming of an old-time cash register and watched as Hannah accepted her change and a large paper bag.

"There are other things we need to talk about. Other issues at the ranch." The levity was gone from his brother's voice, his pronouncement laced with grim foreboding.

"That doesn't change anything, Nick. It's still a hard no. I'm not coming home."

The refusal was met with an impatient exhale. Jackson could feel the eye roll through the phone.

"He's not even here. I understand why you left, but I have no idea why you're staying away."

"That's the thing, Nick. It doesn't matter."

Without waiting, he disconnected, slipping the phone into his back pocket. The hand that touched his shoulder pulled him into the present. And when he turned, he found himself on the receiving end of a wide-eyed gaze.

"What doesn't matter?" Hannah asked.

"That inquisition. And this one." He pulled the heavy glass door of the pharmacy open and led the way into the bright sunshine, glad to have avoided another barrage of questions. Lifting his hat off his head for a moment, he ran a hand through his hair before replacing the Stetson.

The phone in his pocket buzzed again, but he ignored it, setting his eyes on the café a few doors down.

"You didn't eat earlier," he said as he jutted his chin toward the café.

Her eyebrows rose as she took in his suggestion.

"I didn't take you for the type of guy who would suggest a coffee at Chez Pierre."

"Some would say I'm full of surprises." He grinned.

The last thing he wanted to do was to head back to his motel and sink into the bed alone. His sheets, while clean, lacked the smell of flowers he'd developed quite the hankering for.

"I guess I wouldn't say no to a brioche." She smiled and set the pace toward the café. That was the thing about Miss Boston; she was likely the only girl on the rodeo circuit who even knew what a brioche was. If only Jackson could sort out why that mattered and why he was proposing a second breakfast when the only thing he was interested in tasting was her.

An obtuse waiter seated them near the leaded bay window. In the strong morning sun, her skin was translucent, so pale, he struggled to count the freckles on the bridge of her button nose. She was dressed plainly in a black T-shirt that clung to her curves but did little to flaunt assets that begged to be showcased. Curious, she didn't shy away from his gaze.

"Could you bring us some water?" she asked the waiter, smiling as she accepted a leather-bound menu.

"I'll have a cappuccino," Jackson said, accepting a menu.

"Cappuccino? I didn't peg you as the type of cowboy to drink cappuccinos."

He could swear she was mocking him.

"Well, I'm thinking maybe you don't know much about cowboys, especially if you figured being a team masseuse was a gig worth leaving a hospital contract for."

"Hey!" She raised her hands in mock defense. "I'm not leaving the hospital. It's summer break. I'm testing the waters of sports medicine." Hannah cracked the spine of the leather menu and trailed a finger down the offerings. "I am hungry," she exhaled.

"The eggs Benedict is pretty good. I love the hollandaise sauce here," he admitted.

The strawberry eyebrow opposite hooked in question. "Quite the palette."

"What's wrong, I'm not cowboy enough for you?" He was joking, but deadly serious all in the same breath.

"I hardly think that's the problem."

"So, you admit there's a problem?" Now they were getting to the crux of things.

Thankfully, she looked away, distracted by the waiter.

"Un croque monsieur pour moi, s'il vous plait," he said to the waiter. The server turned a delighted grin at him at being addressed in French.

"I'll try the eggs Benedict," Hannah told him.

No sooner had the waiter left than Hannah launched her question. "You didn't mention you speak French."

"One of my many talents," he admitted, biting the inside of his cheek. Why was he showing off? Pulling out all the stops; worse, leaning on his fancy Hartmann education in the hope it might impress her? Miss Hannah Bean was precisely the kind of woman he couldn't make any promises to. She was exactly the kind of woman he couldn't pursue.

She snorted.

Chez Pierre was a cute café. One of the only places in a five-mile radius that served a decent French roast and their duck confit was outstanding. But this? Bringing her here? It was a bad idea. She was going to read it the wrong way, and that was his fault.

"About last night…" she started, raising a heavily fringed gaze to look into his own. "I had no idea who you were."

He wet his lips, nodding in an effort to give her enough space to say her piece.

"What I mean is I— I mean…obviously, we… I mean…"

She was adorable when flustered. "You mean now that we're working together, I should delete your number?"

Her relief was palpable, and his stomach twisted with an unfamiliar pang of disappointment.

"You don't need to forget my number. I'm your masseuse now, so if you need me for anything…" The fringed eyelashes blinked rapidly and she thrust her chin outward as though the action would punctuate her offer.

He grinned.

"For anything masseuse-related," she amended.

The arrival of their breakfast, the second meal plated before him in the last forty-five minutes, relieved her from having to further extrapolate.

"I'll keep that in mind, ma'am."

"My number?"

"Your job." He grinned again. Truth was, while the typical burly masseurs were indeed effective at working out the aches and pains after a day in the arena, it might be nice to try a softer touch. In any case, it was safer this way. Work only.

"I guess we'll be spending a lot of time together then," he said.

"Looks that way. I'm here to do whatever Rodney decides."

If he hadn't been looking for it, he wouldn't have seen it. Another brief flash of color as she spoke about HotRod. Jackson shook his head. His mentor was crotchety, but Jackson supposed there was a charm in there somewhere, evidently. Maybe it was the way he made fast friends with everyone.

"Whatever Rodney decides?"

Hannah channeled a disproportionate amount of focus to her eggs Benedict. "Well, I want— I need a really strong letter of recommendation. And if he, Rodney that is, would be amenable to elaborating on the more therapeutic elements of my work, I could probably leverage this experience into a fellowship, or at least a talking point in my next interview."

He felt it then. The tightness in his throat as he watched her stutter with a ridiculous reason for wanting what could only be explained as a step back professionally. She definitely had a thing for HotRod. Sure, it was difficult to understand how women went for the rough-around-the-edges cowboy, but they did. Jackson had never been bothered by it. Until now.

"I'm sure you'll manage to get all the things you want. You seem to be quite a persuasive young lady."

"I wasn't persuasive enough for you—not last night at least."

Whoa, that came from left field. "I beg your pardon?"

"I just meant I don't always get everything I want."

The thick choke in his throat began to subside. "Is that so?"

His croque monsieur lay untouched before him and by reflex, he picked up half of the fancy-pants grilled ham-and-cheese sandwich and bit into it, all the while maintaining eye contact with Miss Bean. "Well, the circuit's just beginning."

He blinked at the sudden rush of attraction. What was it Rodney said? Ten weeks. He swallowed. A man could do anything he put his mind to for ten weeks, even dampen raging fires and twisting nerves.

It was easy not to think about Nick. It was easy not to think about his dad. Easy not to think about the blood oath he'd sworn: never to have a family. Earn glory for himself, and outshine his father without the Hartmann support. For a moment, it was almost easy not to think about all the reasons he shouldn't be sitting there, having brunch with her.

If there was one thing he knew how to spot, it was trouble. And this five-foot-two masseuse was all kinds of trouble. He leaned into a deep drag of coffee and swallowed it along with the realization that this was one kind of trouble that could sink him. Hannah Bean was precisely the firecracker he couldn't light. And precisely the one he wanted to play with.

Four

The First Cut Is the Deepest

Hannah's feet padded the pavement in a comforting rhythm. It was four thirty in the morning, way too early, but she couldn't sleep. And if she wasn't asleep, she might as well run. And if she had to run... Better to avoid an audience as her jiggly bits wobbled with each step. Grimacing, she renewed her promise to stop reaching for the bread at every meal. Still, running felt good, jiggling be damned. A moment of calm before the storm. She was sure of one thing: with Brad Hill riding rodeo tonight, a storm was in the making.

At least it was flat in Great Falls, she told herself. Her phone beeped. Finally, it was time for her five minutes of walking. Run five minutes, walk five minutes. Who would've guessed she would become a slave to an app? If only bread wasn't so tempting. Silencing the timer on her phone, she couldn't help but pull up her DMs.

Brad: So you couldn't wait for me to call?

Hannah: Calling is overrated. I prefer massaging.

Brad: A different sort of calling...

Hannah: It's a tough job, but someone's gotta do it.

Brad: If it's gotta be someone, I'm glad it's you.

She hadn't answered the last text. How do you answer a six-foot-three-inch cowboy spouting such sweet nothings? *If it's gotta be someone, I'm glad it's you.* That man was 100 percent trouble. Trouble was, she had no idea if he was serious. And now that he was her client and the most important rider on her roster, Brad Hill was out of bounds. Showing her dad she was the kind of girl he could be proud of was immeasurably important. The last thing she was going to do was let her father down by sleeping with one of his crew.

Her five minutes of walking were over and, all too soon, she resumed her race pace. Wobble, wobble, wobble back to her motel room.

She hadn't called Emily. Hadn't called her mother. Hadn't breathed a word about Brad or what her first working brunch had entailed. She couldn't now; not since finding out the reason she'd been hired was to massage the one man who could distract her from her goal.

If it's gotta be someone, I'm glad it's you.

Damn. How to catch a cowboy indeed.

The horizon was lit with pinkish-gray rays and she felt the light warm her. Her entourage was gone. If ever there was a time to be honest, it was now. And if she had to rub down a cowboy?

She was glad it was him.

"You seen the masseuse?" Jackson stuck his head through the doorway, his question filling the interior of the team trailer. Will and Mikey were playing cards, smoking and tossing crumpled bills on the table beside the discard pile. The two riders slept in a different trailer, with Rodney, Jackson and Hannah getting the privilege of a motel room for every city stop.

"I see your twenty and raise you a groom."

"Loser preps both horses? Not likely. I fold." Mikey tossed his cards with a defeated flip onto the center of the card table.

"I haven't seen her," Rodney answered over the betting.

"A bluff? You *bluffed* against my flush?" Despite himself, Mikey reached to examine the hand to which he'd acquiesced.

"The trick is knowing when to spot a sucker." Willie laughed.

"I just need to know if any of you have spotted the masseuse," Jackson repeated, making every effort to keep the edge from his voice. Her mandate was to warm him up, a hard task to accomplish while in hiding.

"I have a name." The Bostonian voice caught him

unawares once again. It came from somewhere behind him and he spun in search of its source.

He squinted, her profile backlit by a strong evening sun. "Hannah," he said as he tipped his head in greeting.

She kicked her foot in his direction and then stepped back from the cloud of dust she'd angered. "Guilty."

Oddly, he was the one feeling guilty. Guilty that he hadn't yet taken her up on her services after a week of gentle offers, confusing personal and professional needs and the blurred line in between.

Jackson jumped down from the trailer and took a step toward her. She was dressed in a white V-necked T-shirt, the thin cotton clinging to her curves, paired with tight, slim-fit blue jeans and the sort of boots only a city slicker would confuse for rodeo attire. It was definitely feeling altogether too personal today.

"I've been looking for you," he admitted, moving closer to her as he stated the obvious.

"I haven't exactly been hard to find. You could've texted."

"Maybe I'm too old-fashioned for that." He lifted the rim of his cowboy hat and grinned at her while issuing a quick nod.

"There something I can help you with?"

"No, I feel ready for tonight." That didn't exactly explain why he'd come looking for her.

"Not really tonight. Don't you go on in forty minutes?"

Glancing at his watch, he clenched his jaw. "Yep. I'm pretty much ready to ride."

She crossed her arms in front of her and kicked another patch of dirt. "So, what do you usually do before you ride?"

He noticed—hard not to—there was a faint blush coloring her cheeks, and it was delightful. "Come on, I'll show you."

In a few short minutes, they'd rounded the corner of the parking lot, heading in a beeline to the stables. "The stables? Isn't that a bit predictable?"

"Careful, you'll come off a bit ornery. Little predictable for you big-city types, isn't it?"

"Quite the vocab for a rodeo rider. Did you go to finishing school?" She laughed and the musical tone hit him in the gut.

"This way, ma'am." He ushered her through the gate into the barn.

The barn smelled like wet hay, earthy and warm. More than that, it smelled like home. At least, the only home that had ever felt *right* to Jackson.

She stood, two feet in from the door, taking in the busyness of the space. Horses stamped in stalls, stretching necks over low railings to nuzzle for treats. Cowboys twisted and wound rope, polished saddles and forked hay, and three chickens clucked their way in and out of the barn as though they owned it. Home indeed.

"I'm not sure what I was expecting, but it wasn't this."

"They don't exactly have a massage table," he confirmed.

She turned, eyes wide as she surveyed her surroundings. He tried to imagine how she must be seeing the place.

"Sorry for the smell." He shrugged.

"No, I like it."

Her admission was shy but, if anything, he related. "Outlaw is this way." He took a few steps toward the center of the barn.

"Outlaw?" She paused, a flash of uncertainty flickering on her face.

"I rescued him. He was wild. A Pryor mustang. My horse." The last qualifier was a point of pride. Outlaw was a specimen, wild yet tame. Ornery yet loyal.

He didn't need to call Outlaw. Just the sound of his voice had his stallion coming to nuzzle for oats. "Sorry, buddy. I just came to introduce you to a girl."

Hannah was beaming. In the low light of the barn, it was impossible not to notice the sheen on her eyes. Good, she liked horses. He still wasn't sure why it was important to him. The why didn't matter just then, as he had a look at her inching toward the stall.

"Brad, you gonna sell him or not?" The rough voice carried through the barn, bouncing off the aluminum gates and echoing.

"Not." Brad was talking to the horse, but loud enough to be heard by everyone in the barn. He didn't turn to address the inquirer, keeping his attention on Outlaw.

"Wanna bet?" The querying cowboy took several steps closer to them, the rim of his hat shading his features.

"Not a betting man. I only like winning," Jackson countered.

"We'll see about that. I'm riding tonight."

He turned. Carter Jones tucked his thumb behind his buckle and stood with his hips thrust forward. Jackson studied Hannah as she studied the man, frowning in her evident distaste of his rival.

"Isn't it getting out of fashion, wearing a buckle you won four years ago?" Jackson couldn't help himself.

"You know, if you're looking for sure money, you could off-load that criminal horse of yours." Carter laughed and spun, boots clicking as he walked to the exit of the barn.

"It's Outlaw, not criminal," Hannah shouted at the retreating man. Carter waved off her annotation, not stopping to acknowledge the correction.

"Now you've met Carter," Jackson said, reaching into the pocket of his leather jacket and digging for any stray treats.

"Why does he want to buy Outlaw?"

"Maybe one day I'll tell you." Jackson winked. In a game of give-and-take, he wasn't about to give anything away in the first few hands. Truth was, he wasn't even sure why he had shown her Outlaw. She was a massage therapist, along for the ride. His horse was irrelevant.

"Carter, eh? I guess I should count myself lucky *his* manager wasn't looking to supplement a benefits package." She reached a hand forward tentatively, hovering above Outlaw's neck.

"You can pet him. He's more calm when I'm around."

"And when you're not around?"

The woman was sassy, he'd give her that.

"Planning on visiting my horse when I'm not around?"

"We'll see."

"Boston, you better be careful. Some people might think you like playing with fire."

* * *

Maybe that was exactly what she was doing. Playing with fire. As Hannah sat in the arena, squeezed beside her father, whom she had yet to confront, she gripped the aluminum railing and leaned forward, as though the new proximity would better convey her support for Brad.

This arena couldn't be more different than inner-city Boston. Or the women's shelter she'd moved into at sixteen, freshly emancipated from her mom. Her current surroundings were also in stark contrast to the buzzing hum of an ER, or the high pressure of an ambulance interior. This arena, and lifestyle, was as foreign to her as her own father, which was precisely why she was here now. To learn.

"To earn any points—" Rodney started.

"Points means money," Mikey interrupted.

"As I was sayin', to earn any points, rise in the ranking, they gotta stay on eight seconds."

"Okay." Eight seconds didn't seem too long.

"Not that okay," Mikey said. "I took a nosedive right over the horns earlier. Stayed on four seconds."

"Right, but you're a crap rider," Rodney added.

"Is Brad good? A good rider, I mean." She couldn't help herself. It shouldn't matter if he was good or not. It had little bearing on why she was there. To meet her dad, get him to like her, approve of her, even. She sipped her Bud Light and smiled at the cowboys next to her. Clearly, her dad loved the rodeo, so asking about it seemed a sure way to melt the ice.

"Brad's more of a horse whisperer. He was breaking horses when I met him, hired him to keep up the stallions back when I was trading in horseflesh."

"I didn't know you did that." Her plan was working. Sure, they were talking about Brad, but she was learning about her dad.

"Don't anymore. But the rodeo circuit was a great place to sell horses, 'specially Montana wild. That's what Brad trained. Wild horses culled from the reserves. Didn't get top dollar unless you managed to break and train them."

"Why did you stop?" Her question spouted from a natural curiosity.

"Brad. Best horses are around the Yellowstone, but he wanted to find a way to stop going there."

Rodney straightened in his seat and drained his can of beer, crushing it before he allowed it to fall to the ground. She willed herself not to ask why someone would rather climb on top of a bucking bull than scout horses along the banks of the river.

"You didn't ask why?" She couldn't stop herself.

"Doesn't matter why. He'll make more money in the rodeo. Me too."

"So it doesn't matter why he rides. Just that he rides."

"He's good. To answer your question, he is real good." Mikey gave her a quick succession of winks.

"Yep, that about sums it." Rodney signaled to a woman carrying a tray of Buds, buying a round for the boys on his bench.

"He startin' soon?" Willie asked.

"Three minutes," Rodney said.

"Go, Brad!" Her voice added to the support screamed by the crowd. His event, bull riding, was last. It was the last, but also the most popular.

"I'll say this, kid's got no fear."

"What do you mean 'no fear'?" Hannah asked Rodney. She'd come tonight because Rodney had asked her to. But as she waited for Brad to ride, she swallowed the conviction she'd come for another reason altogether. To see Brad in his glory.

"Bull riding. Lotta folks would say that's the most dangerous event there is. Need to have ice-cold nerves before you get on the back of a bucking bull, nothing but heart to set you apart."

She didn't like that. She didn't like that at all. Hannah gripped the railing until her fingers felt numb despite the sweaty heat. Despite all the animals and people, the arena didn't smell like the barn. It didn't smell safe.

"He's there, in the chute." Rodney gripped her arm and she followed his pointed finger to see Brad swinging his legs into the chute. If possible, the din of the crowd rose to an even higher, excited, frenetic pitch. Lively music blared, echoing through the stadium, and lights flashed. Over the music, she heard an announcer running down Brad's stats, and the formidable stats of the bull he had just hopped on.

"I don't think that I can watch this," Hannah mumbled more to herself than for Rodney's benefit. But Rodney tightened his grip on her arm.

"Watch him. This is where the kid shines."

Fighting the impulse to correct her dad, insisting Brad Hill was 100 percent man, she nodded. It didn't matter. She doubted she could look away even if she'd wanted to.

"Scootch," Willie ordered, sliding in next to her on the bench. "A minute now, right, Rod?"

"Any minute." Rod bobbed his head toward the chute.

Everything went quiet. For a moment, Hannah didn't hear anything apart from the beating of her own heart throbbing in her ears. In what felt like slow motion, the gate opened and out stormed a bull with corded muscles bulging. The bull wasn't happy, and it bucked, kicking its feet into the air with an anger further fueled by the crowd. But Hannah couldn't watch the bull. She watched the man.

Brad's back bent with the fluidity of a wave, arching and torquing with each aggressive protest from the bull. One hand raised high in counterbalance, Brad leaned. She vaguely remembered her first lesson in bull riding, spouted by Rodney as he explained why access to a good massage therapist was critical. Riders can only touch the bull with one hand. They had to stay on, squeezing the bull between muscled thighs, gripping the saddle horn in a duet of balance and strength.

Beast, the bull Brad was assigned to, had been ridden eleven times. Only five cowboys had managed to stay on for four seconds. What made her most nervous was the reaction of her father, white-faced as he watched the dance before them.

"Six…seven…" the crowd chanted. At eight seconds, Brad flipped off the front of the bull in a twisting hop. A neat sidestep and he was off, to the crowd's roaring appreciation.

Then Beast rammed him and Brad crumpled to the dirt.

Five

Adrenaline

Adrenaline triggers the following changes in the body: increased heart rate, redirected blood flow to the muscles, causing a surge of energy or shaking limbs, a relaxed airway that might cause breathing to become shallow. She knew it all, had studied it, but now she *lived* it.

"Move, move!" Hannah shot forward, ambling her way through eight people crowded around Brad.

"Let her through," Rodney's voice called out and, just like the parting of the Red Sea, the men stepped aside.

There was no miracle, just Brad, crumpled on the dirt floor of the arena.

He was unconscious, his dimple hiding in his slack face as he lay despondent. She pressed two fingers under the ridge of his jaw, finding his pulse steady, a discovery that steadied her own. She lowered her cheek to just above his nose, standard practice to feel the heat and exhale. Instead, she was greeted with a faint but sure inquiry.

"Are you gonna give me CPR or what?"

Hannah snapped back her head so quickly her neck creaked.

"Not today, cowboy." Her voice was thick, and she zeroed in on Brad, who was pulling himself up.

She pushed against his chest. "Stay still. I need to check you out. You could've hurt your spinal column, maybe some nerve damage. That was quite the throw."

"It was a charge, not a throw." Despite her protests, he got to his feet, his hands rubbing his lower back.

"I forgot, you're the expert. I'm just a highly trained medical professional, what do I know?" She was annoyed, but her annoyance was tempered with relief. "Hasn't it occurred to you, if you die, I'm out of a job?"

With a pained expression, he swooped forward in a shallow bow. "I promise to do my best not to die then, if that pleases you."

"What would please me is being able to do my job. Can we find a quiet corner to do a proper exam, rule out any contusions or internal bleeding or…" Her mind was racing as she scanned him from head to toe. He looked okay. Better than okay. Kind of annoyingly better than okay, in fact.

There it was, that half smile, half smirk. "I guess I'm just gonna have to please you another time. I've got some prior engagements I can't get out of."

His words flabbergasted her. *Please you another time?* The nerve...

"You're a legend!" Mikey hustled forward, clapping a heavy hand on Brad's back. Brad winced then shook off his enthusiastic mentee. Hannah watched as Brad walked to the edge of the arena. She pushed her hair back behind her ears, telling herself he was fine. She wondered briefly if repeating something enough made it true. She whispered a mantra in the hopes she could will it true.

My mom was wrong. You can't leave a daughter you never knew existed. I deserve this. My plan will work. Brad is fine.

She cast a quick look over her shoulder and calmly took in Rodney scribbling notes in a notebook, eyes flitting to the lit scoreboard. No matter. He was doing his job. Once again, her eyes strayed to the strong back of Brad Hill. CPR indeed.

He tilted his head back toward a small group of persistent photographers. "The media badges won't get them through the gate," Brad mumbled.

The press was waiting to interview the only man to ever stay on Beast for eight seconds.

"Brad, over here!" A man brandished a microphone in his face, which Brad waved away. "Brad, is it true you're riding ten weeks nonstop?"

Even from four feet away, Hannah could make out the questions clear as a bell.

"That's what they tell me," Brad gibed, his voice flush with confidence.

"You trying to hoard some points or what?" Another reporter swung a microphone in his direction.

"Just doing what I'm told," Brad answered, his voice decidedly less amused at the interrogation.

"Quite a ride tonight, Mr. Hill. Any concerns about mounting Beast's brother?" The man looked down at a notepad then, lifting his head back up, challenged Brad with a follow-up statement. "Says here, his brother's name is Mayhem."

"Mayhem. Bigger, badder, meaner than Beast. Heck, what concerns might I have?" Brad joked.

Hannah bit the inside of her cheek, the sharp pain an anchor to the moment. Meaner than Beast? She didn't like that, not one bit.

"Clancy Evans was paralyzed by the same animal. Career over. They call Mayhem the endgame for who-ever draws him," another reporter said.

"Worse than an ended career," Will interjected, cor-recting the reporter. "The man's not gonna walk again. Have some respect."

The reproach did little to quiet the peppered ques-tions.

Brad raised both hands to quiet the crowd. "Y'all are talking about a ride in two weeks. Don't you think we should talk about tonight? Besides, there are lots of bulls at the rodeo. I'm not going to fret about a draw that hasn't been made yet. My chances of pulling May-hem are one in eight. I'm good with that."

For all intents and purposes, Brad appeared calm. Truly unconcerned. Admittedly, Hannah was only look-ing at the back of him.

Mayhem? Hannah swallowed, tuning out the follow-up questions, head spinning. This job was supposed to be cut-and-dried. An opportunity, not more. But it was tough. Tough not to be affected by the bravery of the men she was treating. Of one man in particular.

The area was cleared by neon-green T-shirts, who swept and herded the onlookers away from the enclosure. Then she felt a hand clap on her shoulder.

"What did you think, kid? Addictive, right?"

She turned and met HotRod's appraisal with one of her own.

"I think Cardic would've been better off hiring a staff doctor rather than a masseuse."

Rodney shrugged. "Men can ride through a lot of pain for the right reasons."

The floodlights cast a white glow on everything and everyone. Hannah swallowed the impression she was walking in an overexposed photo or a New Age Snapchat filter.

"Women can handle a lot of pain too." She spoke the truth under her breath, more to herself than to her dad. Right now, the thing she wanted most was a stiff drink.

Rodney met her truth with a gruff laugh. Then he shoved a wad of chewing tobacco between his cheek and gums.

"You know, that stuff will kill you."

"Everybody dies. But that's what makes us cowboys different. And a rodeo cowboy? We're a breed of our own. Not afraid of anything, not even death. We prove it each time we get on the back of a bull."

"Sounds like a lot of words and hot air." She couldn't help herself and kicked up a pile of dust at her feet. "I mean I just don't get it."

"It's your first week on the job. Give yourself some time to understand, and don't be so quick to judge." Rod kicked at the dirt and tucked his thumbs into the loops of his belt. "Still, you gotta admit, it was a nice win tonight. That ride might just get him on the map. No one's stayed on Beast that long, apart from my boy Brad."

Hannah swallowed her frustration. What was it? This incessant need to prove yourself more manly by getting on the back of a bucking bull? It was insane. A death wish wasn't attractive, so she had a hard time assessing the sport as anything but a bunch of yahoo cowboys out tempting fate. They needed a masseuse about as much as they needed a hole in the head. A psychiatrist would be more appropriate.

Her eyes scanned the perimeter, looking for Brad. She was going to tell him. Tell him this sport was nuts. Share her medical opinion, hard-earned and entirely valid. He needed to stop before he got seriously hurt.

She took a few steps toward the main gate then stopped. The thing was, if he stopped riding, she was out of a job, and the few lines of conversation she'd had with her dad tonight were more than she'd had in her life.

She looked up, scanned the perimeter once again. No sign of Brad.

"Have you seen him?" Hannah issued a friendly jab to Mikey's ribs, bringing her back to the present.

"Brad? No." Mikey was well sauced and halfway through yet another beer. "He's getting another buckle tonight."

"Sure. I mean I guess so, right?"

"He beat Carter." Mikey beamed, proud by association no doubt.

At this, Hannah issued her own smile. Maybe she didn't totally understand the rodeo, but she did understand putting men like Carter in their place. Then she cleared her throat. "Actually, I think I might know where he's at. I'll see if I can track him down."

Five minutes should put some distance between her and the arena. The sky was lit by more stars than she would have seen in a year of stargazing in Boston. She sucked in the wet, hot air and exhaled. It didn't take a country girl to tell the storm promised by The Weather Channel was imminent. It didn't matter. She wasn't far from the barn, and she had a sneaking suspicion she might find Brad there.

She found the barn with surprising ease. The door was heavy, but she managed to open it. However locating the lights seemed an impossible task. She saw him staring at Outlaw and breathed a sigh of relief.

"Brad, I've been looking for you." She closed the distance between them with a few swift strides. His frame was a dark silhouette, lit only by the moonlight that entered the barn through the sliver of open door. By the time she stood a few feet away from her cowboy, she realized her audience was not, in fact, Brad Hill.

"Fancy seeing you here." Carter turned to face her.

Once again, she felt the telltale signs of adrenaline kick in, her pulse echoing in her ears.

"I was just looking for Brad." She started taking a step back.

"He likes wild things." Carter eyed the stall where Outlaw neighed.

"I suppose he might. I…uh…don't know him all that well." She took another step back, reaching with one hand for her phone, wishing there was a subtle way she could remove it from her pocket. The previous feeling of safety she had felt in the barn dissipated.

"I'm sure Brad's looking for me. We have a standing appointment after every ride. I need to treat him."

"Treat him?" Carter smiled thinly. "Is that what they're calling it?"

She felt her shoulders rise of their own accord and leaned into the instinct. In the same way that a bird puffs out its feathers to appear bigger, she put her hands on her hips and widened her stance. She wasn't some wild thing that needed breaking and the comment annoyed her. Just like that, she wasn't afraid of Carter, even though she perhaps should be.

"Don't go rushing away, not when things are just starting to get interesting. I reckon most people are celebrating, especially that winner of yours." He advanced, close enough that a hard lean would have him pressed against her. Then she felt it. His hand on her arm.

"Get your hand off me." Her voice was quiet but as threatening as she could manage. Outside, a crack of thunder let out a resounding clap, and a duet of lightning lit the interior of the barn in a flash.

Seizing the moment to distract him, Hannah stomped on the instep of Carter's boot. He released her arm in surprise and stepped back. It was a move that had served her well in Boston, but she hadn't counted on the steel-toed boots. Carter's laugh was chilling.

"You know, I'm gonna enjoy this a lot more if you fight."

"I'm not some horse you can break. Touch me again and I'll press charges."

"That's cute. You think my buddies on the force

would pay you five minutes' heed? Some city girl trying to exercise her cowboy fantasy, they'll say, no doubt.
You know, I could though. I could help you exercise
whatever cowboy fancy you might have in mind." His
laugh dropped an octave to a dark chuckle.

"Right now my only fantasy is that you put your foot
back in stomping range." She took a sidestep, swallowing a scream as a crack of thunder hit again.

"You know, city girl, we could start slow. Just one
kiss."

Then the door opening widened, spilling more moonlight into the dark barn.

"Hey, Carter. What's the matter? You still lusting
after what's mine?" The voice that broke the tension
brought with it a palpable relief.

Jackson had spent the last twenty minutes looking
for Hannah. He felt bad for having so easily dismissed
her concerns regarding his supposed injury. Truthfully,
he could allow for a quick medical exam. Maybe he
could even allow for a second opinion. More than that,
he'd wanted just a quick chat and, for the life of him,
he couldn't figure out why. In the absence of finding
Hannah, he'd made his way to the barn to consult the
one consistency he'd faced in the past ten years. Horseflesh. More specifically, Outlaw.

The summer storm had moved in quickly, breaking
the heat. He'd quickened his pace to the barn, knowing
the animals were afraid of thunder.

But he was surprised when he opened the stable door.
He knew the voice as certainly as he knew the city girl
it addressed. He felt a flash of emotion so primal he

almost didn't recognize it. Jealousy. Possession. Protectiveness. An overwhelming wave of anger and hate.

Even in the shadows, he could see Hannah's back pressed against the weathered boards of the barn, her face pale in the moonlight. And Carter, that brute of a man, was standing in her space. With *his* woman. And while he swallowed the answering question of why he'd think of her that way, it didn't change the fact that he did.

Carter raised both hands and took a small step back. "Brad. I thought you'd be out celebrating."

In three steps Jackson inserted himself between Carter and Hannah. He reached one hand behind his back, putting it on her hip in the hope that she could draw some strength from him. With his other hand he resisted the urge to punch the smug look right off Carter's face.

He felt a cool hand cover his. Hannah's.

"Don't touch her. Not ever. Or I'll end you."

He'd never meant anything more.

The soft hand squeezed his and Jackson felt emotion clog his throat. To think he almost hadn't come to the barn.

"Them's fighting words," Carter ground out. A flash of lightning lit the inside of the barn once again, enough to showcase the calculated gaze issued in his direction.

"They are," Jackson agreed. He meant them too. Threatening a woman in the barn? It was low, even for scum like Carter. "So I better not catch you near her again. You better not touch her, ever."

"You think you're hot, you hobby-riding cowboy, you don't belong here. Don't think we haven't noticed

fancy gear and high-end leather detailing on your kit."
Carter eyeballed Outlaw's stall.

Jackson fought the urge to correct him. He had won
that kit fair and square, but Carter had a point. Even if
he hadn't won it, he could have bought the kit. Heck, he
could have bought the whole barn several times over. He
could even buy the factory that made the leather kit. But
that was the thing about *Jackson* Hartmann. He wasn't
there to buy it, he was there to earn it.

With regret, he dropped the hand behind him and
took two steps toward Carter.

"Whatever, man," Carter said. "Think what you want,
but that filly wanted it, wanted to feel what a real cowboy can do." He left the barn without waiting for an
answer.

Fighting the urge to follow him, Jackson turned his
attention to Hannah.

"Are you okay?" The question was unnecessary. Of
course, she wasn't okay.

"Better, now that you're here," she admitted. Her hand
reached for his again, and he realized being vulnerable
was easier in the dark.

Lightning flashed, followed seconds later by a loud
crack of thunder.

"We're in the worst of it now," he whispered.

She laughed. A nervous, quiet laugh, but one nonetheless. "Why are you whispering?"

"I don't know." He followed the admission with a
laugh of his own. But there was no denying the rising
awareness.

"Thanks for saving me."

Her words were calm, but they resonated. His feet

were leaden and heavy, anchoring him to the spot in front of her as he looked into her unblinking blue eyes. "I have a feeling you would have been just fine on your own, Boston."

Finally, he forced himself to take a step back, putting some space between them. It was easier to have a clear head with a little bit of space between them.

"The guys are going to be looking for me," he admitted. Across the barn, he whistled for Outlaw. "Sorry, buddy, I got nothing for you," he confessed to his four-legged friend. The midnight-black horse neighed in protest and stamped in displeasure.

"Well, we'd better be going then," she confirmed. There was a tone to her voice; a mild disapproval that he couldn't help notice.

"You don't have to come." He spoke the statement to her retreating form, watching as she approached the main door to the barn.

"That's quite the invitation," she countered, spinning to face him.

Her eyes were wide and shining with unspent tears. It was the kind of look that jarred him. The kind of look he couldn't answer to.

"I didn't know you were interested in a different sort of invitation," he muttered. Pushing past her, he felt the heat of her body as he squeezed through the door, only to be met with warm rain.

In a flash, she was by his side. He swore softly under his breath.

"Here, take this," he muttered as he pulled off his

leather jacket. It was well-worn, had been his favorite for over a decade, but it might keep her dry.

"I don't need your coat," she protested even though she accepted it and slipped it on.

"Let's just get you back safe and sound. There's been enough drama for tonight."

Despite her small stature, she fell into pace beside him, matching his stride with two of her own.

"What about Carter?" he finally asked her.

"Carter made it clear to me what the cops might say. Plus, what exactly would my complaint be? That he put his hands on my arm? Not exactly grounds for prison time." She punctuated the observation with an eye roll.

"You know as well as I do, he wouldn't have stopped there."

Her cheeks were wet from the rain, but she wasn't crying. Hannah was calm, methodical and, sadly, absolutely right. He wanted to hug her. Pull her against him in a crushing embrace. Instead, he nodded. "It's your call. I'm just glad I came when I did."

Then Boston did something that surprised him. She closed the space between them.

Jackson didn't move, frozen in place.

Her head fell against his chest and her shoulders shook as she let go of the tension that had coiled inside her. A delayed response. He laid his hands on her back and pressed slow circles between her shoulders. "It's okay to cry," he assured her, unsure of where his capacity to comfort was coming from.

The permission only served to make her cry harder.

Jackson lost track of time. He lost track of responsibility, of angry promises and age-old threats. Gone were vendettas and goals and everything that wasn't her, clinging to him in the rain.

"You know, you remind me of Outlaw." He immediately regretted the confession. *How stupid, comparing a woman to a horse.*

The comparison quieted her and she pulled back just enough to look him in the face. "Why? You want to break me too?"

He raised a hand to her cheek, the pad of his thumb wiping away a tear. "No," he stated, surprised. "The best thing about you is that you *won't* be broken. And your strength? It's damn beautiful."

The rain played its part. Hannah, unfazed by warm tears in a July storm, lifted her chin.

"I can't be strong all the time." Her voice cut him and he felt his stomach twist at her honesty.

"Me neither," he said quietly.

Then, with a flash of lightning guiding his way, he lowered his head and pressed a kiss onto her parted lips.

He meant it as a soft kiss. As a comfort. But it quickly spiraled. Her hands twisted into his shirt, tugging him to her. He cradled her face in both of his hands and pulled her exactly to where he wanted, toward him. His parry was met with hers, and she pressed forward as though to melt into him with a rush of desire for which he was unprepared.

They were interrupted by headlights. She jumped back before the driver of the offending vehicle could disembark. The rude interruption did little to cool his libido, but he did have the presence of mind to be grateful their kiss hadn't escalated in an open parking lot.

"I'm sorry, Brad, that was the picture of unprofessionalism." Her demeanor shifted to cool professionalism.

Just as well. She didn't date cowboys. And he? He didn't date anyone. He couldn't.

Six

Rubbed the Wrong Way

Hannah was magic. Jackson closed his eyes, blocking out the wood paneling of his motel room, and groaned. "That. Whatever it is that you're doing right now, feels amazing."

Hannah pressed the palms of her hands in concentric circles along the base of his spine, or so he imagined. And it felt glorious. "Thank Cardic." She laughed.

"Thank the Lord more like it. My back has never felt better." It was true. The fall last night had looked far worse than it felt, as did most rodeo injuries, but he winced none-theless, appreciative of the added sympathy. He'd felt en-tirely ready to challenge Carter to a fight, and he would have had it come to that. But as of nine this morning, it was forgotten... *All* was forgotten.

Except that kiss.

They didn't discuss it. In an unspoken truce, and to anyone who happened to look, they were the picture of professionalism, client and masseuse. But lying there half naked on her massage table, he couldn't forget their kiss. Not when she was torturing him with a touch so exquisite, he recited the alphabet backward in his head to avoid his body betraying precisely how much he was enjoying her attentions.

The bottle of oil let out a squelch as she spat more onto the center of his back. Then her fingers, cool and sure, spread the oil.

"Your back looks like a Picasso."

He could only imagine the smattering of colorful bruises. He'd been spending afternoons with Outlaw, and the stallion had been in a mood lately. Not to mention Beast. Or Viper. He was perhaps not the best judge of next steps with his animal counterparts. Nonetheless, her concern was misplaced. He wasn't looking for someone to worry over him. Those were the types of people he tended to let down the most.

"Art connoisseur, are you now?" He groaned again as she leaned into her work, running both hands up the bottom third of his spine.

"Hardly, I live up to the doctor stereotype of illegible handwriting, and my drawing is even worse." She spoke through her motions, maintaining a delicious pressure. He felt her touch everywhere.

"I highly doubt that," he breathed through another groan.

"I look like an artist? That sounds like code for ugly."

"Hardly," he reassured her, mimicking her own intonations. She couldn't be further from the truth. He'd said artist, but what he'd meant was art. She had the look of a marble statue, carved with Renaissance curves and mouthwatering proportions. Not that he'd studied art.

Jackson's phone buzzed. He raised his head, wincing under the weight of his own thoughts. Nick's name and number flashed on the screen thanks to caller ID.

"You want to take that? I can wrap up here."

He wished he could erase the polite professionalism in her tone. Then he swallowed the flash of desire, reminding himself that Hannah's professionalism was needed. He could hardly take his massage therapist for a roll in the hay. He wasn't ready to pay too much attention as to why he'd succumbed so entirely to her kiss last night. It would be too easy to blame her wide eyes and luscious curves, the femininity that drove him to distraction. No, he'd withstood pretty women before. She was more than that. She was *Hannah*. But it didn't change facts; she was on Cardic's payroll. And she was not the kind of woman looking for a quick wham-bam-thank-you-ma'am. And he couldn't offer more.

"No, it's not a call I need to answer," he said.

She didn't respond; instead renewing her circles on his lower spine, her fingers getting closer and closer to the waistband of his jeans. Jackson pressed his forehead into the massage table, grateful she couldn't see him bite his lip. He wouldn't be flipping over anytime soon.

"What does that even mean?" she asked, interrupting a few minutes of silence.

"Nick. We used to…" He paused. How could he explain Nick without explaining Jackson? Without explaining himself? "We used to work together," he admitted. *Work together.* It was honest. Hartmann Ranch was hardly a family home, definitely more of a family work unit—at least the way his father had run things.

"Work together."

"Work together," he affirmed. Lifting his head again, he swung an arm from the side of the massage table and reached for his phone. Scanning the home screen, he read the text message that dinged, frowning.

Jacks. The horses crossed the Yellowstone last night. They are migrating off the reserve. We need to have a plan for how we're pitching this to the livestock commission. Current commissioner is not in our pocket.

Horses? Nick must mean the mustangs.

"So?" Hannah pressed.

"I should probably call him back." The admission had a cost. She pulled her hands away from him and, just like that, the magic spell she'd cast over him, moving both hands in constant streams around his back, was broken. But more concerning? What was up with the mustangs?

"You don't have to go," he mentioned, not meaning it. He didn't want an audience for this conversation. His ruse was but another reason why he couldn't get involved with anyone, not on a serious level. Keeping a secret was a lot easier when you had only yourself to trust.

"Yes, well, for our sessions to be more effective, we should cap them at forty-five minutes, and perhaps repeat them a little more often. Tomorrow, we can do a morning session, then again after lunch before you train."

Tomorrow. So he wouldn't see her until tomorrow. He swallowed as he reached for his shirt.

"Right, tomorrow it is." Tonight he had a thing anyway. But should he invite her? No. Best not to mix business and pleasure. Her massage therapy sessions were doing a fine enough job of blurring those lines.

"Sure," she said. He caught her then, staring at him as he pulled on his shirt. He paused before doing up the last few snaps. Her eyes were heavy on his chest, and he could feel her rake his skin with a weighted gaze that felt hypnotic. Until his phone buzzed again.

"I guess your coworker really needs you," Hannah noted, shoving her oil bottles into a gym bag and pulling at the zipper.

Damn it, Nick, this better be urgent.

His eye caught the clock by the bed. Their massage session had gone on for an hour and twenty minutes, though it had felt like seven. Seven minutes of heaven.

"Till tomorrow morning then," he told her as he nodded.

"We'll see." She winked.

His clever retort was interrupted by another call.

"What?" he barked at his brother, his mood soured by her departure.

"Nice to talk to you, too, Jackson. Why aren't you calling me back? There's a lot happening here."

Jackson closed the door Hannah had left open behind her, and paced back into his room, grabbing a beer from the minifridge under the TV console.

"If I wanted to talk, I'd have called you back." Jackson popped the tab on the beer and indulged in a re-freshing gulp.

"Yeah, I figured. But what about if I want to talk to you?"

Nick was infuriating.

"Wasn't that the whole point of the power of at-torney? You're meant to decide for me, and send the checks. Speaking of which, I haven't had many of those lately." Jackson took another mouthful. He battled a small feeling of guilt. It wasn't Nick's fault that he didn't want to go home.

Nick was pretty much the only reason he *would* con-sider a visit. Nick and Amelia. The changes were un-deniable. Nick had found Rose. Amelia—commonly referred to as Mia by her family— had moved home to manage the resort branch of the business. He could argue they were changing the face of Hartmann Ranch, and the unfamiliar feeling that he was missing out was getting tougher to tamp down. But Brad Hill didn't belong at Hartmann Ranch, and Jackson Hartmann couldn't win the PRCA championship. He couldn't give his father's ghost the satisfaction of seeing the Hartmann name in lights and glorified, but the chance to win his dad's most prized possession, the PRCA buckle, and on his own merit, was too tough to ignore. He'd ride—and win—as Brad Hill.

"Yes, I can vote for you when needed, but there's a lot going on. We're making changes here. Things aren't like they were." Nick's voice sounded hopeful. That wouldn't do; Jackson couldn't allow him to have any hope he'd go back. Brad couldn't.

"Nothing can change enough, buddy. I'm not coming home. I've closed that chapter of my life."

"Can you hear yourself? You can't close the door on who you are, *Brad*."

The insult stung. Nick was the only one who knew his alias. He'd been the one person Jackson had confided in precisely because Nick wasn't the sort to use an alias as ammunition. At least until now.

"Is that why you're calling? To give me some sort of morality lesson or—" he rubbed his chin and frowned "—advice? Because, to be honest, Nick, I don't want either."

His rebuke was mean, but Jackson never pretended to be a good guy.

"I'm gettin' real tired of being the bearer of bad news, man. I feel like I'm fighting for a legacy no one wants. You haven't even come back to see Rose since we got married. Or Alix, your niece, for that matter."

"You got me there, man. But at least I met *Mary* when she came to the rodeo." He grinned despite himself, wondering if Nick could hear his grin through the phone. When Nick had hired Mary, a British nanny, to take over the education of his niece Alixandra, he hadn't known he'd in fact hired Rose, who was filling the shoes of her recently deceased sister. Jackson had met "Mary" before she'd admitted to being Rose, and now he felt a kinship with his sister-in-law. They both knew the duality of living a lie.

"Look, things are going well, but I'm trying to be the kind of guy that admits when he needs help. I don't want to take on more than I can chew, and compromise what I've got waiting for me at home at night. Not to mention, it's different now. I have a wife. Still feels like an out-of-body experience to say it. But, man, she's everything."

"Trying to drop your apple a little farther from the tree, is that it?" Jackson headed to the bathroom and turned on the shower, letting the water heat up before he hopped in.

"I'm trying to plant a new orchard," Nick corrected, albeit a little dryly.

"If you're looking for help planting, I'm more of a horse guy—"

"That's exactly why I'm calling you. We've got a problem. The mustangs are migrating onto the plains north of the Yellowstone. A new herd, and the commissioner wants to cull the colors that aren't original. If we don't do it, they'll send in a team. Ryan's guys."

Ryan Stuart was the wildlife commissioner, and his crew had the reputation for rerouting stallions off private land and into his own corrals.

The horses were *Jackson's* legacy, not his father's.

Pryor mustangs were indigenous, and the original colorways were valuable. There was a market for wild stallions, but a purebred would fetch the highest price at auction. Mustangs migrated, so letting the wildlife commission onto Hartmann land could serve to just chase the stallions off the boundaries and into state parks. It always came down to money.

"When's this?" he asked, trying to force casual into his tone.

"Inside the season. They head out in twelve weeks if we can't prove the herd on our land is in keeping with the species mandate. You know as well as I do, if they call open season on the mustangs, it's gonna be overrun. I'd rather sell off the land than let that animal hunt on Hartmann acreage."

"There's one thing we agree on." Steam filled the bathroom and Jackson frowned at his clouded reflection in the mirror.

"I have the PRCAs, then I'll come home." He ended the call without waiting for Nick's reaction. He'd explain later that he'd come for the mustangs and then leave. Let his brother feel this win, however temporary.

For now, he had a sponsorship party to prepare for. He wouldn't think about the quick flash of relief he felt when he said the words aloud. *Then I'll come home.*

"What do you wear to a sponsorship party?" Hannah felt insane asking Emily to offer advice on an outfit over Zoom. "The little black dress feels like a classic, but I'd rather be unexpected."

"Wear the pink thing."

"The lingerie?" Ha. Not likely. She'd packed it as a joke, but now the underwear mocked her.

"Yes! Exactly. Wear that to a roomful of cowboys and car execs. Lingerie for the win." Emily clapped her hands together excitedly. "I wish I could come," she lamented.

"You *can* come." Hannah offered the invitation but even if Emily left right now, there was no way she'd arrive in time.

"Ha, not quite. This Cinderella has a hot date with more bedpans." Emily fanned herself with a worn paperback, thumbing through the pages for a little breeze. The Zoom call went static, the video freezing and offering the perfect opportunity to read the cover of the book she was fanning herself with. A Western romance novel. Hannah grinned.

"How about this?" Hannah suggested, more to herself than her counterpart, when the screen unfroze.

Holding up the emerald dress, she wondered if it was too casual. It was silk, but a handkerchief design, large squares of fabric looping off the neckline in an asymmetrical drape. Casual but sexy. Hopefully not too sexy for Dad.

"I love that color on you," Emily said, "but I'm still voting for lingerie."

Hannah sighed. "All right, I'll wear the lingerie if it will shut you up. But I still need to pick a dress."

"Yes!" Emily squealed. "You totally have to do that. I always feel more prepared for social occasions when I'm appropriately clothed."

"Right. Except that I don't need to be properly clothed *underneath* my outfit."

"That's what you think," Emily teased.

Hannah drew her lips into a thin line. She didn't just think, she knew. Rodney had been the one to invite her tonight, and she wasn't going to lose focus. Tonight was a chance to get to know her father better.

"You talked to Amy lately?" she asked, hoping her tone was okay. She didn't want to taint the question with any of her disapproval and color her friend's opinion with her own.

"Amy? As in your mom, Amy?"

Yes, technically Amy was her *mom*. She had hardly set the bar high for her dad. "Can you think of another Amy we both know?"

"You gotta admit it's weird you call her that."

"Weird for who?" Hannah hung the green dress on the back of the bathroom door and rummaged through her makeup bag. Time to dedicate herself to putting on the mask. It was easier to like pretty people. That was as sure as science. She couldn't morph into a lithe stick figure, but she could optimize the assets she had.

"She's fine. I saw her today. She asked about you."

"I hope you didn't tell her about Rodney," Hannah uttered quickly as she put on her mascara. "Ouch," she exclaimed. Served her right, she'd stuck the wand in her eye. That was the worst kind of pain, the kind you inflicted on yourself. The kind you couldn't blame on other people.

She studied herself in the mirror over the dresser in her motel room. No, that wasn't true. Having someone you love hurt you was far worse.

"Relax," Emily assured her. "What shoes are you wearing?"

"Not your smoothest transition, Em." Hannah grinned. "But you know I love talking about shoes. Check these out." She kicked a foot up onto the bed, in view of her laptop's camera. Nude stilettos with the elegant arch of a four-inch heel.

"Those are high," Emily accused, jealousy evident in her mundane criticism.

"My cowboy is tall, so it doesn't matter," she blurted.

"*Your* cowboy now, is he?" Emily teased. "This from the girl who doesn't kiss cowboys." She laughed.

And that was the problem with having a best friend who remembered every offhand comment you made. Emily didn't hesitate to throw her stupidity back in her face.

"I gotta go. Rodney's picking me up in twenty and I need to do my hair first." Without waiting for an answer, perhaps swept up with a wave of embarrassment she didn't care to examine overmuch, she slapped her computer shut. Tonight was about her and Rodney. And yes, there *might* be a chance she'd cross paths with Brad. After all, it was a Cardic Motors event. But this extra effort she was making to look nice wasn't for him. Maybe if she said it aloud, she'd believe the lie.

No sooner had she rimmed her eyes in black kohl than there was a knock on her door. She opened it, only to flush red. "Brad," she managed to say, glad her brain was functioning well enough to work out his name.

Brad Hill was dressed in a slim-cut navy suit. The fabric skimmed across his shoulders, the cream dress shirt buttoned to the neck and trimmed with a bolo tie. She had always thought bolos were girlie. But Hannah was ready to admit when she was wrong. On Brad, the accent was intoxicating.

"Y-you aren't who I was expecting," she stammered.

"Says the goddess," he teased, smiling wide.

"What's that supposed to mean?" She felt both flattered and insulted, an unbalanced feeling that warmed her.

"It means you look good. Too good." He added the qualifier, a little darkly, under his breath.

She felt her mouth curve into a half smile despite herself. She shouldn't be pleased by the revelation, or by the fact that for some reason, he fought their attraction too. Quite frankly, she was in disbelief that he'd even pretend to think she was a goddess.

"Lemme get my purse," she muttered, spinning on her heels and grabbing her clutch.

Closing the door to her motel room behind them, Brad offered his arm, which she took. For balance, she told herself. Only for balance.

It was impossible not to ignore the spanking new truck in the motel parking lot. Shining white, with black accents and an oversized cab. "That's yours?" She nodded at the vehicle.

"For now." He opened the door for her and tipped a navy hat in her direction. "Ma'am," he said with a grin.

It was hard not to grin at this vision in emerald.

"Thank you, sir," she returned with exaggerated emphasis on the *sir*. "This truck smells fab."

"It smells new," he agreed, missing only for a moment the smell of his old ride. His antiquated truck, Bessie, had smelled like hard-won rides, horses, hot leather and sun-cracked gear.

They rode in silence.

"It's about twenty minutes till we get there." He felt the need to break up the quiet with a mundane offering.

"Twenty minutes," she agreed, pressing her palms flat against her dress. "I wasn't expecting you to pick me up," she finally admitted.

So that was what was on her mind.

"Who were you expecting?" The question was obvious, but he found himself holding his breath in anticipation of her answer.

"Rodney."

"HotRod? Right, he was already in Billings, so it was faster for me to get you. He asked earlier, and I'd said it wasn't a problem, but I guess I could've checked with you. I'm sorry if the disappointment is too much to bear."

"I'm not disappointed," she promised.

"I keep thinking about Carter. About last night. I shouldn't have just let him walk off like that." He kept his eyes on the road during his confession. It felt easier that way.

He could feel her stiffness at the mention of his name, and swallowed the regret at having introduced the loser into their conversation.

"No, you did the right thing," she assured him.

"Sure doesn't feel that way now." He chanced a side-long glance and noticed the pink flush that warmed her cheeks.

"It was the right call. Guys like that... I mean...what could you do? Beat him up? Feels a little high school."

"Hey, that's the Wild West you're talking about," he chided. But he was smiling. Their kiss in the rain had been worth giving up the satisfaction of pummeling Carter. Plus, there was always next time.

"So, how are you liking the new job?" He changed the subject with practiced ease.

"It's fine. Good, even. I don't know. I wasn't expecting to like it."

So she liked it. Liked him, too, maybe. That was good, even if it shouldn't be.

"What have you been liking?" He danced around the real question. *Do you like me?*

"I wasn't expecting to like cowboys quite this much," she admitted.

He lifted his foot off the gas pedal, the truck slow-ing in response. Taking his eyes from the road for just a moment, he wondered… "What's all this hate for cowboys? I gotta ask."

The blush was impossible not to notice. He would have seen it even if he hadn't been looking for it. The color started at the base of her neck, climbed to the apple of her cheek. Maybe a gentleman would have changed the subject. Too bad there weren't any of those in his new truck.

To his relief, she didn't shy away. Instead, her chin jutted forward and she squared her shoulders. "My mom had a thing for cowboys."

"I'm taking it you don't want a 'like mother like daughter' reference," he noted.

"Ha. Understatement of the century. Or maybe not. Maybe describing her as my mother is the understatement of the century."

Jackson reached for the radio and cut the sound. Listening to pop hits didn't seem appropriate given her disclosure.

"Birthing vessel? Feral parent? Feels closer to the truth than the moniker of momma dearest." Her tone was bitter, each biting admission spat with anger.

"Well, you turned out okay. At least there's that." Turning his eyes back to the road, he rubbed the supple leather of the steering wheel pensively.

"No thanks to her."

"Your dad then?" he pressed, unsure why he was digging. This line of inquisition was firmly beyond the therapist/client discussion points. Despite himself, he wanted to know. Had to know.

Gone was her blush. She stared out the passenger

window, robbing him of the opportunity to admire her profile. "I didn't know my dad. At least, not until recently."

Her voice was quiet and Jackson got the point. He was surprised she'd admit all this in the space of a few minutes.

"I didn't know my dad very well either. Bitter man. He left for seven years when I turned ten."

His truth must have surprised her. Her shoulders pushed back and she straightened in the seat. "At least he came back."

"He tried to make up for lost time and 'turn me into a man.' I always found hypocrisy hard to respect."

"Yeah, nothing less manly than running out on your family."

He swallowed. "You got that right."

She reached for the knob and turned up the radio, humming to a top-ten tune as it screamed through the speakers.

Just as well the music filled the truck. He couldn't stop listening to the one thought echoing through his mind. *Nothing less manly than running out on your family.*

Was it what he was doing to Nick? In an effort to be different from his dad, had he turned into the man he despised the most?

Seven

All That Glitters

"I didn't even know there were this many people in Billings," Hannah admitted, taking in the glitterati on the scene. People milled in and out of each room, the attendees dressed in all things vogue.

"I admit I wasn't exactly expecting this either," Brad said.

As she looked around, it didn't take Hannah long to put her finger on the unifying quality of the guests. An apparent black-and-white dress code.

"You look really nice," he added, perhaps interpreting her evident concern at having arrived in an emerald dress. Of course, she was wearing green. She was always dressed wrong. Try as she might, she would never quite fit in.

"I guess I didn't get the mémo." She shrugged, hoping her contrived nonchalance would cover some of her embarrassment at being the only woman not wearing black. *I should have worn the little black dress. Damn it, Rodney, this was precisely the sort of information that generally made it onto the invites.*

"Don't be ridiculous. You're like a Pryor mustang in a sea of farm animals." His comment was off the cuff and as she raised an eyebrow in his direction, he revised his compliment. "I mean you look great. Better than great."

The party was being held in a gallery. A converted sawmill turned art house, the single-paned, hammered-glass windows spanning floor to rafters. The ceiling was open, with raw beams exposed and encircled with twinkling fairy lights. And the flowers… They were opulence personified in five-foot arrangements of white calla lilies and peonies. For a moment, she was starstruck by the beauty of it all. By the sheer grandness of the décor.

She noticed Rodney making his way to them.

"May I present Brad Hill." Rodney bowed, sweeping his cowboy hat off his head as he introduced Brad with a flourish to the licensing team at Cardic Motors. Hannah watched the interaction, feeling like a fly on the wall of a very fancy party. Like a fly dressed in a green dress.

"Much obliged to meet you," Brad replied, lifting his hat off his head in a polite nod. He was taller than all of the Cardic execs, but it wasn't just his height that gave him an air of authority. Hannah studied the other men, who were, in her opinion, a little too clean. A little too slick. Then, of course, there was Rodney.

Her dad was predictable, and it was somehow comforting. Black jeans, black boots and a black dress shirt embroidered with red twisting roses and bedazzled with silver snaps and studs. His outfit looked more like a cowboy costume than a black-tie outfit, but it did provoke a smile from the exec team they had set out to impress.

"You sure know how to work a crowd," she muttered under her breath. Rodney didn't hear her above the guests and the music.

"And who might this be?" A suit to her left raised a glass of champagne in her direction.

"This is the most important person on our staff," Brad said. "Hannah Bean, staff masseuse. She manages the injuries before they become incapacitating."

"I used to think the only reason to ride in a rodeo was to meet a nurse, but I now stand corrected," another suit added, a grin on his face. "A staff masseuse is a compelling argument indeed."

"Lots of reasons to ride," Brad corrected, "and while Hannah certainly makes the harder side of rodeo a little softer, there is something about the challenge I've always been drawn to. Taking on a bull can be a good way to test your mettle."

It wasn't lost on her, the way his explanation sounded like a challenge. From the stiffening posture of the exec, it hadn't been lost on him either.

Brad's hand landed on the small of her back. A featherlight touch she might not have noticed had he not been all she was able to think about. It was her anchor, that light touch on the small of her back. She leaned into it and felt a stroke of his thumb in answer. Both torturous and glorious. And impossible.

It occurred to her, not for the first time, being a massage therapist didn't garner quite the respect the profession deserved. She felt Rodney's eyes on her and stilled. Did he know what was happening behind her? No, she was overthinking things. Rodney had no way of guessing at Brad's touch. It was more a gesture of support than anything suggestive anyway. She was *definitely* reading too far into things.

"You don't say." Suit One smiled into the ongoing conversation around her.

"I—I am learning so much. Being on the road with the team is a huge opportunity." She hated herself for the stammer and smiled through it.

"Didn't realize there was a lot to know in massaging?" Suit Two winked at his friend and the two tittered. There it was again; a lewd stare.

"Excuse me, but Miss Bean has a degree in medicine. She took this position—"

"I took the position as I was thinking about a minor in sports therapy. And I had ten weeks before my position at Bozeman started," Hannah cut in, shooting him a sharp glance. She didn't need saving. She wasn't alone in a barn, she was in a sea of businessmen, where her wit should suffice as all the protection she needed.

"Sports therapy?" Suit One chuckled.

Hannah smiled. That got their attention. While she hadn't sought a medical degree for the respect it earned her, she didn't shy away from flashing it when needed either. "Yes, the high-impact nature of the strains and torque stress makes for a very interesting case study. And who knows how long the fans will salivate over their beloved cowboys getting beat up, so the longevity of the findings or their relevance in sports therapy is admittedly beyond me." She laughed, but forced coolness into her reaction. "For a summer, I welcome the experience. The academic correlations are unquestionable." *That should do it.*

"*You're* the Cardic-sponsored masseuse," Suit One interjected, his tone imbued with the threat. Some men didn't take well to standing corrected, even when the rebuke was subtle.

"Definitely a reason I signed with y'all. Looks like a few of you are dry, why don't I head to the bar and get some refreshments?" Brad broke the tension with the offer of drinks, and the exec team shook their heads in unison. "I'm a full-service cowboy."

"We're all drinking Bud Light," Suit Two said. "And why don't you get a Zinfandel for the lady?" He winked at her and Hannah felt her ovaries and everything female in her body recoil. Then she recalled Brad's last comment. A full-service cowboy? Why had she gotten the distinct impression Brad had meant that comment just for her? Just like that, her ovaries slid right back into place.

"I'll have a—"

"Mint julep?" Brad winked at her then leaned forward to whisper, "I rather like the effect they have on you."

"A glass of white will be fine," Hannah confirmed. She needed to show Rodney she was the daughter he hadn't known he'd always wanted and starting them down the mint julep rabbit hole could prove dangerous.

"White, the color of surrender. I'll take that too," Brad whispered in a tone only she could hear. Despite the entourage, she couldn't fight the feeling they were

alone. The directness in his gaze made her feel naked.
And seen. At least if she were naked, she wouldn't be
wearing the green dress…

"It'll take more than a glass of wine for me to surrender." Hannah winked without meaning to, turning her
head in a rubber-necked reaction to check if inquiring
eyes had witnessed her slip. No, she was safe.

"Let's start with one glass and see where we go, shall
we?" Brad grinned, his dimple peeking back out as if
to flirt with her.

"If it means you'll be getting me a drink before I turn
fifty, I'll take it." She turned, squaring her shoulders to
the rest of the group.

"If you think I'm letting this one out of my sight,
you're mistaken," Brad added, slipping his arm into
the crook of her elbow and steering her away from the
rest of the men.

"Thanks," she added when they had put more distance between the licensing team and themselves. To be
fair, she wasn't even sure what she was thanking him
for, the utterance a reflex.

"Don't listen to those guys. I think getting more experience in the sports industry is smart. You'll see a lot
of injuries before you set foot in the hospital as staff."
He was talking to her, but she couldn't stop looking at
the stretch of shirt pulled against his muscled chest. It
would be easier to chat like this had she not had her
hands all over him that morning. Had she not explored
the hard expanse of muscle for herself, in an entirely
professional setting, of course.

"Yes, right," she managed to rasp out though her

mouth had turned suddenly dry. "You know I've set foot in the hospital before, right?"

"I don't doubt it."

They had migrated to the back corner of the room and now found themselves beside the harvest table laden with hors d'oeuvres. This was no backcountry hoedown. The food was just pretentious enough to signal the money that had likely been thrown into this event. Foie gras; endive salad arranged onto platters of bite-sized amuse-bouches; crostini topped with roasted goat cheese; honey-and-fig, dry-rub short ribs on silver saucers with shaved carrot adding a punch of color to the plates.

"All this, and they don't put out napkins." Brad whistled.

She laughed. How could she not? "Worried about getting a little sauce on your fingers?" She reached for a rib, making quick work of the hors d'oeuvre. Then, as though issuing a dare, she offered a finger covered in barbecue sauce to him. Two could flirt. *Take that, cowboy.*

Quick as a flash, he grabbed her wrist with his free hand, angling her away from the crowd. Momentarily frozen with shock, she moved under his guidance. He had taken the bait and she didn't know what to say.

When his mouth closed over her finger, hot and wet, her stomach flipped. His tongue swirled around her finger, licking, savoring, and she couldn't help it. Flashes of that tongue tasting her breasts, her thighs, played out before her and she had all to do not to moan with pleasure. It couldn't have been more than a few seconds, but for a moment she felt frozen in time, focused only on what his mouth was doing to her. Then, grabbing hold of her sanity, she looked away, desperate to see if his action had been witnessed by her dad. Brad was standing too close to her, and she felt aware of every inch of his body, as though the air between them was static and buzzing with electricity.

"Coast is clear, if that's what you're thinking." He spoke gruffly then bit his bottom lip. What was he thinking?

"Do you really think anyone here gives a hoot about my medical opinion?" It felt easier, somehow, to question his beliefs than to confront her own. Namely, the importance she not fall for a cowboy, which right now was in serious jeopardy.

"You make me feel a lot better. I know we haven't had many sessions, but really, you have worked miracles," Brad assured her. He hadn't moved; she was still only inches away.

"Well, thank you."

She scanned the room, wondering where Rodney had disappeared to. He was the reason she'd come, not to listen to sweet nothings from this cowboy. She'd been doing her best to get to know her dad, even if it meant stalking the diner to ambush him at breakfast. Or spending free moments in the trailer learning the finer points of poker. Still, it was working. He'd smiled this morning and slid into her booth before asking to join her, which had made things feel natural, almost normal.

"I think we should find the others," she suggested, hoping her request sounded casual enough. She watched the muscle in Brad's jaw tighten as he gritted his teeth and swallowed.

"Right, sure. He's probably near the money."

"The money?" She'd asked the question and followed it with a deep breath, aware of his eyes on her chest as she inhaled.

"I bet he's working on pimping me to other campaigns. HotRod gets a cut of all my bookings." He took a step back, and she exhaled. It was easier to breathe with more space between them.

This was new information. She'd known Rodney did the negotiations, but she'd thought he should, given the kinship between them. It wasn't hard to guess at the loyalty Brad exuded. After all, he didn't need anyone making bookings for him. Fans were falling over themselves after each ride, begging for autographs. Hannah couldn't imagine procuring a booking would be any more difficult than a simple phone call, so why did Rodney hold the spell over Brad?

"Why's that?" Sometimes the easiest way to get information was to be direct.

Brad grasped her by the elbow and guided her with gentle pressure through and around people she didn't know. He glad-handed as needed, but kept them on a forward trajectory. Once past a group of women in their fifties, each fawning over Brad's recent win, Brad answered. "I've been with Rod a long time. I wouldn't have had any of this," he said as he gestured around the room, "if he'd left me in the barn where he found me."

She thought his comment odd. He didn't seem to want any of this.

"Brad," another woman called out for him, "you were amazing last week. Thrilling watching you ride."

Brad tipped a hat in her direction. "Ma'am, thank

you for your support." He kept his distance, continuing to push forward toward the opposite end of the room.

"I've been looking everywhere for you two," Rodney complained as he approached them. The executives must have left because Rodney awkwardly juggled several bottles of beer before setting them on the tray of a passing waiter. All but the one he kept for himself.

"Looking for us, were you?" Brad took his hat off and ran a hand through his hair. "Yeah, you know I hate these events. When can I go?"

They had convened near the tables; a series of round, counter-height, Art Nouveau bar tops housing bouquets of white tulips. Nearby, a four-man band played acoustic iterations of classic rock, and Hannah was grateful for the music. It made it more difficult to chat and easier to zone out and focus on the men before her. Brad leaned on the nearby table, frowning at Rodney. The wall behind them held the biggest screen Hannah had ever seen, featuring a video loop of off-roading trucks speeding on dusty fields, parking with a flourish against a riverbed where men fished. She could guess why they wanted Brad signed on for their sponsorship. Nothing sold the masculine vehicle better than the ultimate outdoorsman. There was a refined rugged quality to Brad that would make excellent TV. Heck, they might even start selling more trucks to women.

"Buddy, you got to sing and dance just like the rest of us. You're the most important person in the room."

"Are they gonna get you to do a commercial?" She interrupted the conversation.

"No. I'm not doing that," Brad answered succinctly.

"Actually," Rodney said, "they're gonna film a few shorts. Something to run around the PRCA finals."

"That's not in the contract." Brad glowered.

Rodney waved at a server passing by them, holding a silver tray high above her head. More of the endive amuse-bouches.

"Sweetheart, where are you going with all that?" Rodney snagged three and ate them all when Hannah and Brad declined. "Thing is, the commercial technically is in your contract. Right after the 'other marketing possibilities' subclause."

The glower deepened, and Brad straightened, pulling his shoulders up and looking every inch of six foot three. "I told you from the beginning I wasn't doing any shorts. No TV, and nothing national."

"Look, Brad, it was in the contract. Go read it. You don't even know what's good for ya. Look around, buddy. Cardic doesn't offer sponsorship deals to just anyone. I got you all this." He gestured around the room. "And you—" Her dad issued the command in her direction. "What's wrong? You never heard of a little black dress? And would it kill you to flirt a little with the people paying your bill?"

"My services don't include flirting." She defended herself through gritted teeth. Without thinking, she put her hand on Brad's arm, as though her touch might hold him back from a more aggressive follow-up.

"Perfect. I hired the only masseuse in Montana who won't flirt." Rodney managed to make the statement sound like an insult.

"What you hired is a massage therapist. Per my contract." Brad's hand was back, and she felt its steady pressure as she navigated the encounter. It was surreal. Her dad had become the bad guy, and the cowboy a knight.

Rodney had finished chastising her and turned back to Brad. "So you *did* read the contract, or did you only read the part you cared about? This is exactly why I introduced you to her at the same time I told you about the deal. You're predictable, kid."

"I wonder if you can predict what will happen to you if you keep up with this," Brad said, his voice low, chilling.

Rodney shrugged, unaffected by the threat. "Have a drink. We have work to do."

"I don't think so." Brad stood his ground. "Look, Rodney, I would have preferred not to do this here, but I suppose it's just as well you know before you get too invested in any other possible opportunities for me. After the PRCAs, I'm out."

"Out?" It was Hannah's turn to be shocked. It shouldn't matter. After the series, she was out too. Eight weeks and she'd be in Bozeman, doing the medicine she'd trained for. Hopefully, updating her dad weekly on the status of his daughter's sparkling medical career, the prospect of which seemed less likely after tonight.

"Leaving at the crest of your career? Over a misunderstanding?" Rodney looked shocked.

"Some things are more important."

What was more important to him than rodeo? And why did she care?

"Like family? Like the supportive family I've always been to you?" Rodney played the only card he had. It might've been a more effective trump had he not already shown his hand.

"That's rich, buddy, because I don't think you'd screw your family over like this. I said no TV. I told you from the start I'd like to keep my mug off the national lens."

"A face like yours is made for TV," Rodney insisted, swigging back the rest of his beer.

"That really isn't for you to say now, is it?" Brad insisted.

The server bumped into Hannah on her second pass of the back corner. This platter had white wine and, in the absence of the mint julep, it seemed a good idea. She took two glasses, passing one to Brad. He didn't even notice, so she put a hand on his shoulder. The effect was immediate. He turned, his warm, honey eyes finding hers. Once again, the static electricity buzzed between them.

"I need to go to the bathroom." She didn't know another way to stop the argument. Watching the two men size each other up like street dogs was horrifying. Even worse? If it did come to a street fight, she wasn't sure which side she would root for.

"I'll escort you," Brad said. He was predictably courteous.

"Tell the Cardic guys I said bye," Brad called over his shoulder to Rodney, who stood sulking.

In no time, he led them across the room once more, pausing in front of the ladies' room.

"I don't really have to go," she admitted.

"Yeah, but we really have to go." He smiled. "I've had about as much of this party as I can stand."

"Well, you're my ride, so I guess we'll leave together."

She wished for a minute that her voice was a little less breathy. A little less obvious.

"Before you leave, you want another rib?" He traced one finger along the length of her index, with an excruciating pace.

Want another rib? Did she ever.

Eight

The Longest Ride

Jackson hadn't thought it possible to hate a new truck. Especially this new truck. It might have been top-of-the-line, with all the bells and whistles, but none of that mattered. He hated it. That new-truck smell used to be intoxicating but now it was sickening. The only good thing about the damn truck was that Hannah was in it. And, by the same token, being near her served only to remind him of the things he couldn't have. He wasn't the love-'em-and-leave-'em type, but neither did he want anything more. One thing for sure, he wouldn't end up anything like his dad, chasing pretty skirts across state lines, family be damned.

When Jackson was ten, his dad had walked out on

their family. For seven years, his grandmother had stepped in to do the heavy lifting with the parenting. All because his father had chased a skirt. Jackson would be better than that. Better than him. He had to be.

"Are you really quitting the rodeo?" No sooner had she buckled in than she asked the question. Her wide eyes focused on him, but all he could see were her freckles. The moon offered the ideal filter, bouncing off her white skin; she was luminous.

"Yeah, Nick needs me." It was a poor excuse. After all, he had no intention of settling back at Hartmann Ranch. Nor did he want to grow roots here.

"Your coworker?" she queried, propping her feet up onto the dash.

Did the woman remember everything? He cleared his throat. "Sure." Executing a tight four-point turn, he changed gears and left the gala behind them. Maybe it had been a bit rash, advising that he would leave the rodeo, and to his agent nonetheless. But the notoriety he was earning was dangerous. He didn't want to risk being recognized by the wrong people. The kind of people with connections that could force him home. Or worse, the kind of people who were *related* to him.

"So eight more weeks?" She interrupted his thoughts.

"Don't worry, Boston, I can get thrown off a lot of bulls in eight weeks. Aches and pains are guaranteed in my line of work. You'll be busy, and that's a promise." He rubbed a hand across his jaw before replacing it with a slack pressure on the steering wheel.

"I wasn't worried," she said, her voice barely above a whisper. Her foot tapped against the dash, the staccato pace belying her nerves.

"I'm sorry about tonight," he said simply, not bothering to dress up the apology with pointless exaggeration.

She shifted in her seat and put her hands in her lap. "What do you have to be sorry about?"

"Now there's a loaded question." He smiled. The smile was a mask for the twisting conscience roiling in his gut. What did he have to be sorry about? Lying. Letting her think even for a minute he was the kind of guy that could give her what she deserved.

She thought it. He could read her thoughts as clearly as if they had been written in his own hand. He was feeding the fire, and he knew it. What he couldn't do was get his head around how to stop. He couldn't remember ever wanting a female this bad, and there was only one way he knew to get over it. Over her.

"Trying to dodge the question, are you?" She pushed for her answer.

"I mean..." He let out a low whistle. "I'm sorry for Rodney, sorry for the suits, sorry for everybody looking at you like a piece of meat tonight."

"That's not your fault." She dismissed his apology, waving it away. Jackson pulled his attention from the road and watched as she twisted a loose lock of hair around her finger. He was consumed by the motion, perhaps all the more so because she was unwittingly enchanting him.

"Suggesting you should flirt with those guys like he somehow owns you, it's disgusting." If he hadn't wanted to quit rodeo before, seeing the presumptuous orders dripping from Rodney's lips had been the final push. Sure, he and HotRod had a history, but it was time to write a new future. He didn't want any part of a team that spoke to Boston like that. She, or any woman, for that matter.

"Rodney is not the first guy to think his agenda was more important than anyone else's."

"That's an odd way to put it." Jackson slowed the truck. He wasn't driving the speed limit, nor did he want to. He was acutely aware that the sooner he reached their motel, the sooner he would be saying good night. This was how he found himself rolling at sixty miles an hour on an eighty-mile-an-hour stretch of highway.

She reached for the radio. "Do you mind?"

"Course not, your pleasure is my pleasure." *Your pleasure is my pleasure?* How much wine had he drunk? One glass and he was talking nonsense. It felt easier to blame the wine than to admit he'd voiced his own feelings.

"Eight weeks then. You'll be done when I'm done. This is kind of like expiration dating but without the dating." She rushed the modifier, blushing.

"Not sure I know what expiration dating is." He kept his eyes on the road. Avoiding eye contact was the only sure way to avoid a blush of his own.

"It's when you go into something, knowing it'll have an end. Sometimes, you try things you wouldn't otherwise try."

"Oh, I get it. Expiration dating." He nodded.

"I didn't mean you and I should…do that. I meant like, that was funny because, I am your massage therapist and, like, we know it's good and…and we almost, you know when we were out that one time, and your stopping—" She was babbling and it was adorable.

"Maybe we should." He pulled into the motel park

ing lot with heaven-sent timing. Jackson put the truck into Park and turned to look at her. "Expiration date," he finished.

She didn't say anything. He watched as she swallowed. In his experience, the silence was a good thing. Hannah had to be thinking about it if she wasn't outright refusing.

Expiration dating sounded like exactly the kind of dating he was ready for. They'd both know when it was over, and commitment was out of the question. It was a way to have his cake and eat her too.

She unbuckled her seat belt and retucked the loose strand of red hair behind her ear. "I don't date cowboys," she said.

"Right. I remember. But you just said that expiration dating was all about doing things we wouldn't otherwise try."

"How do you know I haven't tried dating cowboys?"

"We're addictive." He grinned. She blushed and looked anywhere but at him, eyes flitting around the interior of his truck. *This is going to be fun.*

Without answering, she reached for the handle of her door, opening it into the cool night air. In a flash, he was out of the truck, offering a hand to help her step down from the cab. He took another step toward her, and another step into her space, sparking the electricity once again.

"If you're so addictive, then how am I gonna quit you in eight weeks?"

"That's easy," he replied as he took another step toward her. "I'm gonna quit you."

"You're not at all worried? Not at all worried that *you*

might get addicted?" She took another step and lifted her chin, so close he could swear a deep inhale was all he needed to bring their chests together. He abstained.

"That's the thing about expiration dating, right? We both know now what it is. Dating with all the frills but none of the pain."

"None of the pain," she repeated, eyes widening. She nodded, a brief flash crossing her eyes that he pretended not to notice.

If pain was the cancer, then she was the cure. He breathed. The kind of breath that heaved his chest and made them touch, made them want. Then she repeated the move from the bar, the same move he'd been reliving ever since, waking in the morning raging hard at the mere thought of her breasts pressed against his chest and arms wound around his neck.

"Then kiss me, cowboy," she said as she smiled. It was that half smile he'd caught a few times. The type of smile that indicated there was a little piece of happiness missing. But it didn't matter. He was missing the same thing.

He started on her shoulders, both hands roaming over but barely touching her skin. She was soft. So soft, he could hardly bear it. Bringing his hands back up, he followed the line of her neck to cradle her head. Then, pulling her head to his, he pressed his lips to hers, finally indulging in a taste.

Her lips parted with little resistance and, as she opened to him, he pressed for more.

"I've wanted to do this since that night in the bar." The admission felt easy now; now that he was kissing her.

She didn't answer. Instead she rose to the tips of her

toes to meet his parry with one of her own. Releasing her head, his hands roamed her body, skittering down her sides, past the curves of her hips. It was impossible to rein in his need of her, but he reckoned he better try before it was too late.

"I better go," he managed to drawl between kisses. He'd never meant anything less, and the words sounded so hollow, he was embarrassed to have said them. But he'd leave if she wanted him to, of that much he was sure.

"Not likely. If we've only got eight weeks, we'd better make the most of them."

Relief rushed through his veins.

"Your pleasure is my pleasure," he said with a smirk, unrelenting in his roving exploration of her lower back.

She pressed forward once again, deepening her kiss before pulling away abruptly, separating their bodies.

"We'll see." She winked.

The green squares of fabric danced as she turned abruptly and walked toward the motel door.

"As hard as it is to say goodbye, I gotta admit I love when you walk away." Sure, it was a cliché, but clichés were clichés for a reason, and damn, did she look good sauntering off.

"Walking away? I thought I was *leading* the way."

Slack-jawed, he bobbed his head. "Wild horses couldn't keep me."

"Just give me two minutes," she whispered, her voice breathy.

Pressing the fob of his key chain, the beep-beep hastened his step. Expiration dating. Could it be the answer?

He supposed it depended on whether he was asking the right question.

* * *

It was a lot easier to fake being confident than actually being confident. What was it Emily was always saying? *"Faking it" and "having it" often look the same, at least when addressed with a cursory glance.* That was the thing though. She had a sinking feeling there would be nothing cursory about tonight. It was definitely a bad idea. But he didn't know anything about expiration dating. She could package the experience however she wanted. She was the one explaining it, so she could make her own rules. The idea gave her confidence and, for a second, it occurred to her she'd have to fake it a little bit less than she'd feared.

He knocked. Because that's just what he did. Brad Hill was the consummate gentleman.

"Room service," he called to the door. If he was room service, she loved the menu.

She had two minutes. Two minutes to decide how ready she was to fake it. In a flash of indecision, she hesitated. No, she had to do it. Had to pretend to be the most confident woman in the whole world. Not a brazen buckle bunny. She wanted to be the best version of herself tonight.

She opened the door then took three steps backward, leaning away from his reaching hands.

"Uh-uh-uh." She shook her finger at him. "I think before we fall down this rabbit hole, we better go over a few ground rules."

"Ground rules? I better sit down for this." In four long strides, Brad Hill flopped onto her bed then pulled himself up into a seated position, bent forward and rested his arms on his knees. "Give it to me then."

Be cool, Hannah, be cool. She smiled. "Thing is, we gotta keep it a secret. You see, with expiration dating, if other people know, it can get kind of awkward."

Brad didn't say anything, just nodded. His tacit agreement gave her the boost she needed.

"And you gotta be nice—"

"I'm nice!" At this he protested.

"By *nice*, I mean we each have to try. This is expiration dating, not expiration friends with benefits."

"Honestly? I'm not sure I understand the difference."

"The difference is no other people. Like…" She blushed. "Like if you need to, you know, get tested, so we can…not worry but still be safe."

Mercifully, he lifted his hands and stopped her. "Okay, you got it. No one else. That's fine, Boston. And I've been tested. I'll do it again or whatever you want." He laughed.

"It's not funny. I'm not just some woman you picked up in a bar." She flushed, praying her naïveté was less obvious than she feared.

"No one's saying you are." Gone was the smirk. He was all kinds of serious.

"Right, so yeah, you don't tell anybody, and it's a complete secret. And when it's done, it's done." One thing she was sure of, Rodney could never find out, especially after tonight.

"Looks like someone's gonna date a cowboy after all." He stood and took a step toward her.

"Expiration date," she corrected breathily.

"Yep," he noted, bending to plant a kiss just under her jaw.

This was either a terrible idea or an amazing one. He

followed the first kiss with a second, and she flushed. *An amazing one*, she decided.

"You done negotiating?"

The third kiss melted into the fourth and she tilted her head back.

"Done. Yes, I'm done."

"Good, because I'm just getting started." Kisses five and six trailed down her neck to her collarbone.

He slid the strap of her dress over her shoulder and pressed a kiss where it had been, repeating the action on the other side. Her heart hammered in her chest as he pulled her dress down. For a moment, before she could stop herself, her hands raced to her breasts to pin her dress in place.

"What?" He stopped his rain of kisses, looking up at her in confusion.

Emily and her stupid, stupid ideas. Because, of course, she was wearing hot-pink lingerie. She couldn't look more as though she'd prepared for this. Like she'd somehow planned it. It was humiliating.

"I—" She didn't know what to say. What could she say?

"What? Something wrong? You want me to go? Hannah?" He peppered her with questions, tempering them with soft kisses on her shoulder.

"No, I'm just embarrassed."

"Embarrassed?" He met her discomfiture with a shy smile. "What could you be embarrassed about?"

Another kiss, this one on her collarbone. Then she stepped back. Time for big-girl panties indeed.

Releasing her dress, the flowy garment slipped off and pooled at her feet. She straightened, faking confidence as she bore her hot-pink corset, laced in a sheer mesh, complete with matching garters and barely-there panties.

"Hannah Bean." He let out a whistle and she willed herself not to blush. "Are those for my benefit?"

"No."

But her protest didn't land, and he laughed. "If this is your laundry day, this whole expiration dating concept is going to be amazing."

She lowered her hands, pushed back her shoulders. Now was the moment for confidence.

He whistled. "You look good enough to eat."

It was her turn to feel relieved, and she allowed herself to smile, not sure she could stop herself even if she needed to.

"Good enough to eat?" She took another step toward him and once again they were linked with the electric energy she'd felt all evening.

"Precisely. And I'm starving."

He bent his head to hers but she backed up, pulling her lips from his reach. "You are wearing far too many clothes."

"I'm afraid what's under this shirt is hardly as appealing as what you're serving. Not to mention you've already seen the goods."

Instead of answering, she set about unfastening his buttons, her hands focused and nimble. He discarded his suit jacket and kicked off his boots, and before she knew it, he was only wearing a cowboy hat. Hot damn, it was a lot of cowboy.

"If I don't taste you, I'm going to explode," he whispered into her ear, biting her lobe as though the nip of teeth would accentuate the sentiment.

"Buffet's open," she breathed.

He needed little encouragement and pulled her to him, spinning her to face the wall. Sinking to his knees, he pressed a kiss into the side of her knee, then another farther north. She wondered, for a moment, if she would be able to stand still as he focused his attention on her most sensitive areas.

"These are pretty, but I'm thinking I'm gonna like what's underneath even more," he said as he toyed with the garters and panties. The scrap of fabric offered her what little modesty she'd hid behind.

With a hand on each leg, he widened her stance, and she complied. She felt his breath on her then a sweet pressure on her hips as he guided her to the bed. She fell into it, the new posture affording him access to a deeper exploration.

Time faded as he pressed on, touching her, kissing her, playing with her and winding her like a coiled rope.

"Are you having fun?" she panted, her hands pulling off his hat then twisting in his hair. She was.

His answer was a renewed effort, the mix of fingers and hot breath a torturous combination. Before, she'd been filled with concerns. About her father's judgment of her and about making better decisions than her mother. But now Brad Hill had dispelled those concerns with a few well-placed swipes of his tongue.

Now all she could think of was him. All she could feel was him.

She squeezed her eyes shut, the crescendo of tension rising in her. His ministries were practiced. You didn't get to be this good on your first walk in the park, she realized. No, she couldn't think of that now. Instead, she focused on his breath, hot against her. His hands, sparking electric current through her. The focus offered a welcome relief.

He moved down to her hip, pressing a kiss into a dimple there.

She was acutely aware that from this angle, she didn't boast the same washboard six-pack as her rugged counterpart. She had more of a keg, and despite a lifetime of resolutions, the soft tummy was ever present.

He clicked his tongue and pulled at the sheer fabric. "I love this."

"This?" She choked. "Tell me you're not referring to my wobbly bits."

She blushed. *Nice. Way to bring attention to your worst attributes.*

He rubbed his chin from the base of her bikini to the curve of her rib. Then repeated the path with a series of kisses. "You're beautiful. Every bit of you. Soft. Womanly." He punctuated every phrase with a wet kiss. Brad was a gorgeous man, but in that moment, he'd never been more attractive.

"Still, I'm going on runs, working on it." She didn't know why she felt the need to make excuses.

He caught her wrist, flipped it and pressed a kiss to the inside of her hand. "Whatever makes you happy, but try to stay a little soft, I'll make it worth your while."

So he is perfect. Basically, perfect.

His hands pushed hers away and, with a maddeningly slow approach, unclipped each hook of her corset, pressing kisses onto her skin as he uncovered it.

Instead of answering, she twisted her hands in his hair. It was easier than saying something clever. The kisses relit the fire in her belly, and she pulled him by the shoulders on top of her. If she was soft, he was hard. Hard in all the right places.

She closed her eyes, as though removing the one sense would heighten the others. As she forced her eyes to remain shut, she felt everything in slow motion. He pressed his forehead against hers, offering a brief reprieve from his kisses. He smelled like liniment oil and peppermint. His hands, callused and rough, were sure as they gripped her.

Pulling away from her, he reached for his pants, cast aside on the bed.

"What are you…?" she started, before realizing his motivation. Protection. Incredibly, there was nothing further from her mind right now. How embarrassing.

Moments later, he rejoined her; this time, ready to take her.

As he lowered his weight to her, she widened her legs, granting him access. She felt the pressure and lifted her hips to meet him as he entered her. The fullness surprised her. It was both what she'd been expecting and wildly different. It wasn't the first time she'd been with a man, not the second, either, but it was the first time she'd felt so full.

"My God," she said, rocking against him, hands on his hips, pulling him deeper.

He didn't say anything, just pushed farther. Everything about him was hard. Everything about him was more innately male than any man she'd ever been with.

It was like everyone had been doing it wrong, and he had the key to crack the code.

He didn't stop. He feasted on her while he took her, kissing every inch of exposed flesh he could reach. He ravaged her lips with a pressure she feared would bruise.

"I want more," he whispered in a hot breath against her neck. "Closer, come closer to me," he encouraged.

Before she could move, he slid a pillow under her bottom, offering a new angle to heaven. Raking fingers along his back, she felt him go deeper. "Don't stop," she cried, willing this sweet torture to continue.

And continue it did. Again and again, he rode her until their bodies were slick with sweat. For a brief moment, she managed to hope the room next to theirs was vacant, but she hadn't the presence of mind to restrain herself. Then her body tightened. She felt a surge of heat. Of an overwhelming need to cry and scream and be limp but also to arch, every muscle in her body twisting with charged nerves and energy until his lips found her breasts again and she exploded into a million pieces, quivering against him.

His groans heated and somehow her limp body managed to match his, writhing under his hips until his body tightened and he stretched his chin, arching into her a final time. He rolled off her moments later and then pulled her against him.

"That was incredible," she sighed on a shaky breath. "I love how you make me feel feminine."

"You are feminine," he whispered into the back of her neck. "Small, curvy and mine," he added, pulling her closer to him, the round of her ass sliding against him.

"For eight weeks."

"For eight weeks," he agreed.

She'd thought he was going to add something, a disclaimer or perhaps an addendum. After the sweaty sex they'd shared, maybe he was thinking eight weeks wasn't long enough. She felt the same way.

Nine

Broken

It'd been a good long minute since Jackson Hartmann had woken up entirely sated. It was amazing, waking so rested, especially given the lack of sleep. He glanced over at Hannah. She looked younger when she slept, face relaxed, hair lush against the pillow. And those freckles… He was hard just looking at her.

Against his better judgment, he kissed her on the shoulder and she stirred. "Are you waking me up?" she murmured, eyes still closed. Then she cracked one eyelid, lashes bashing. "Again?" The other eyelid followed suit and both eyebrows rose with an inquisitive arc.

He kissed her shoulder then, grinning officially, set about giving her a hickey.

"How old are you?" She swatted him away.

"Just marking what's mine." He bit her on her shoulder, the suction—or rather, the branding—oddly erotic.

"We're expiration dating," she reminded him, swatting him again.

"If you think this hickey is going to last more than eight weeks, you're massively overestimating my abilities."

She turned and the sheet wrapped around her fell away from her body, offering him a clear view of the luscious curves underneath. "Didn't feel like I underestimated you very much last night." She grinned at him.

"Don't start something you can't finish," he teased, immediately regretting the challenge. Didn't matter how good last night was, or how happy he felt this morning, this was going to finish, in eight weeks minus one day. He'd be damned if he'd make the same mistakes as his dad. He wasn't going to promise anything to her. Jackson Hartmann wasn't about to make a single promise he couldn't keep. Sowing wild oats was in his genetic makeup, and though he was ready to fight his heritage as hard as he could, the niggling voice of self-doubt was ever present to remind him how easy it would be to lose it all. Rolling onto his shoulder, he lifted his hand and trailed it down the curve of Hannah's rib cage. Surely there were easier ways to start the day than a punishing round of threats from his inner conscience. Yes, reveling in the satin-smooth skin under his fingertips. He swallowed. Better things indeed.

"What I had in mind shouldn't take that long," Hannah professed aloud, sleepily.

He felt a hand explore along the edge of his thigh and clenched his jaw, willing himself not to react.

"We gotta meet with the crew. Rodney's going over our road plan at breakfast."

The mention of Rodney deflated any feelings of ardor her attentions had provoked. Similarly, she abandoned her endeavor, sitting upright in the bed.

"When?"

"Nine. Only guy I know who insists on meeting on a Sunday morning."

"I forgot." A look of panic crossed her face. "The diner, yeah?" She hopped off the bed, clinging to the sheet. The military corners tucked and starched to the bottom of the mattress wouldn't allow her more than a few steps from the bed. She pinked at the prospect of unveiling her rich curves.

"Nothing I haven't seen before, Boston," he assured her, leaning back against the headboard and propping another pillow behind him to better enjoy the show.

Hannah hesitated, shifting her weight from foot to foot. "Have you no shame? Leave a girl some modesty," she begged.

"I'm amazed you find any time to be modest," he teased, making a big show of covering his eyes with his hands then executing an exaggerated peek through his fingers.

The action was met by a speeding pillow that hit him smack in the face. "Okay, okay, you've made your point!" But his protest fell upon deaf ears as she was already ensconced in the bathroom.

"You gotta leave now," she yelled through a closed

door. "You can't exactly show up to the diner in the same outfit you wore to the Cardic party."

He frowned. She had a point. He stretched and felt his feet tip over the edge of the bed. Funny, he didn't mind the bed half as much with her in it.

"And what if I did?" Just because she had a point didn't mean he couldn't play with her.

She opened the door to the bathroom a crack and eyed him through the slit. He could hear the shower running and swallowed the regret that she should be in it alone.

"All you're doing is wasting time." Her singsong voice carried through the door, and he smiled.

"I'll meet you there," he promised, pulling on his pants and heading toward his truck.

"You're late," Rodney hissed, red-faced and hung over, as Jackson entered the diner.

"You're the one who insists on making these meetings on Sunday morning. Freaking sacrilegious if you ask me," Will mumbled, throwing back black coffee as though it were a shot of whiskey.

"If I need your opinion, I'll ask for it," Rodney snapped.

"Coffee perhaps?" Hannah suggested. She'd arrived before Jackson because, of course, she had. Not only had she been on time, but she'd managed to look fresh-faced and beautiful, not so much as a dark circle under her eyes to betray the sleepless night they'd both enjoyed.

"Make it two." Jackson slid in beside her on the bench. Amazing that he'd managed to arrive late yet still find a seat next to her. Mikey and Will must be slower than he'd assumed.

"You can order breakfast when we're done work," Rodney directed, dismissing the waitress before Jackson had a chance to order the coffees. "We've got forty rides across two state lines. The next eight weeks are critical and I need everyone here to push."

It was a rare side of Rodney, the serious side. He must need the money, Jackson figured. For a brief moment, he toyed with the idea of an anonymous donation. Something to ease the pressure just a little.

"Forty rides? Five a week? Feels like a lot." Will, normally the quiet one in their group, was hardly a complainer. But the guy had a point. Wasn't exactly a lot of healing time with such an aggressive schedule.

"To ride that many events, we're going to be doing a lot of driving." Rodney lowered his eyes and stared at Hannah. "You can ride with me."

"I'm sorry?" Under the table, Jackson put a hand on her thigh. He was finding it difficult to listen to anything Rodney was saying, let alone care about it.

"Your ride? I thought you were in the trailer," Hannah clarified.

"Yep," Rodney replied. "You ride with the team."

"Okay." She chewed on the word as she said it, dragging it out with her indecision.

"Yes, it is. I need everybody on this team to do as they're told and stop questioning my authority all the time."

The rest of Rodney's orders fell on deaf ears. The five of them were an odd bunch, and long-term plans didn't matter much for people who made their living on the road.

"I'm taking the truck," Jackson reminded everyone. "Just gotta pick up Outlaw and hook up the trailer. Shouldn't be a problem."

"When is the first event?" Hannah asked, her hand sliding over his under the table. He spread his fingers on her thigh, to allow hers to intertwine.

"Tomorrow, not so far. A four-hour drive. It ain't bad," said Rodney.

"Well, it'd be nice to settle in first. I'd like to have another look at Mikey's ACL," Hannah answered.

"We can leave right after breakfast. I've got a few strained muscles of my own that might need tending to, sooner as opposed to later," Jackson added. One muscle in particular could use some attention of the female variety. Of the Bostonian firecracker variety, to be more precise.

"Long as y'all are in fighting form tomorrow." Rodney waved then stood from the table. "And I want her to work on you, Brad, properly. You need to be in top form if you're going to ride this schedule."

"Sure, well, since she's here to care for me, maybe she should ride with me. She could work more, tend to my quads more regular like, if we ride together." He was doing it again; that chameleon behavior he despised in himself, where he'd modify the way he spoke to get what he wanted. Exactly what his dad would do, shifting to fit in with other women, with other businessmen, and he hated himself every time he slipped into the bad habit. But maybe a bad habit for a good reason was something he could forgive.

Rodney reddened then slammed his coffee cup

back on the table. Coffee spewed over the edge and he snarled. "Making travel arrangements, too, now?"

"Just looking at what's right," Jackson reminded him. It was surprising, the negativity.

"You do that then, kid. Remember what's right. Remember who got you here…and how." Rodney's head dipped into a curt nod and he left, his heeled cowboy boots clicking on the aged linoleum floor.

"Somebody woke up on the wrong side of the bed." Mikey laughed.

Jackson joined him, relieved if, for once, he wasn't the butt of this joke. It was easier to be relieved when you knew for a fact you'd woken up on precisely the side of the bed you'd hoped for.

Week one of the insane tour passed quickly, Jackson and Hannah falling into a comfortable rhythm. With no further outbursts from Rodney, Hannah's position as copilot in Jackson's souped-up truck was unquestioned. He was grateful for the company, although try as he might, he was unable to learn much about her. And despite himself, he grew more and more curious by the day. They didn't talk about Carter, and they never talked about the expiration phase of expiration dating.

They moved from one motel to another, sleeping together, the second room reservation going unused. He was getting used to her, but that was the point of expiration dating. It was safe to fall, because the safety net was there. When this was done, it would be done, and he wasn't going to be the bad guy. Still, he felt guilty for not telling her who he really was, and guiltier still for not spoiling her the way she deserved.

He was enjoying lying in bed beside her when he heard a sharp knock on his door. He lifted his head off the pillow, taking in for a moment the sleeping beauty next to him. Her hair spread across the pillow like flames of fire but more beautiful. He felt a spark of desire, only to be fanned by the faint groan she let out in her sleep.

Tap, tap, tap. The knocking resumed, insistent and authoritative. Jackson had the feeling it was not a summoning he could ignore.

"Who do we know that would knock at six thirty in the morning?" Hannah groaned, eyes still closed.

"I'm not answering," Jackson confirmed, pulling her back against him, the soft curve of her as addictive as advertised.

The knock came a third time, persistent in its interruption.

"Somebody better be dead," Jackson huffed, pulling himself away from the warm woman at his side and swinging his feet to the ground. He pulled on briefs, but nothing else, unwilling to afford courtesy to anyone who would wake him at that hour.

"Nick," he breathed in surprise as he opened the door to find his older brother. "What the hell are you doing here?"

"I've been keeping up with you." His brother was dressed as he always was in comfortable denim and a tailored shirt, cream-colored Stetson and boots. He looked as though he'd been awake for hours, not a hair out of place, and Jackson swallowed the niggling regret for not having put on at least a T-shirt.

"Kinda got me at a bad time though." Jackson inclined his head toward the bed and Hannah pulled the covers up to her chin, flushed to an adorable shade of persimmon.

"Wouldn't have to drop in on you like this if you'd answer my calls," Nick accused.

Guy hadn't changed much, Jackson thought. Nick always had loved a good lecture.

"Man as clever as you can't work out for himself when a person doesn't want to talk?" Jackson rubbed his jaw and stood there, inviting his brother to leave with a glower.

"When have you ever wanted to talk?" Nick shrugged, unperturbed.

"Exactly." His brother knew full well he wanted nothing to do with the family, yet here he was nonetheless. "What do you want, Nick?" At six thirty in the morning, the best approach was to get to the point.

"That any way to greet your brother?" Nick shot back.

Jackson leaned his shoulder into the frame of the motel door, careening his neck to get a view of his brother's Lexus. "Sorry, Nick, but what did you expect? I don't know how many times I can tell you there isn't anything you can say. I'm not gonna put on a fancy suit and pretend to care about the legacy I didn't ask for." He could hear Hannah's voice echoing a question from behind as she wondered aloud who he was talking to.

"Look, you don't want the legacy, fine. That suits me just fine, but we're blood. And even if we weren't, I can't think of anyone else better suited to take on the livestock commissioner."

"Even if we weren't blood? What are you even talking

about?" Jackson ran a hand through his hair then hissed, "Listen, can we not do this here? Come on, Nick."

Nick took a step back, eyes flicking over Jackson's half naked state and the redhead on the bed. "A groupie?" His voice was heavy with disdain. That was perfect; they were about to settle into the oh-too-familiar chorus of *You could do better*, or better yet, the *I'd always hoped for more for you*, likely framed with a *When will you settle down, Jacks?*

"She's not a groupie," Jackson stormed. "That's my—" He hesitated then leaned in to say, "Girlfriend."

Nick's eyebrows shot up in surprise. "Girlfriend?"

Jackson abandoned the doorframe, taking a few short steps back to grab his clothes. "Gimme five minutes. I'll talk, but I'd rather not talk here."

He'd made the admission quietly, but no doubt she'd heard. He'd have to think of something to say to her, but that was future Jackson's problem.

Ten minutes later, he was showered and dressed and sliding into his brother's Lexus. Hannah had dismissed his explanation, mumbling, "You'll tell me about it, later on. I'm sleeping, babe." The "babe" had been an afterthought, and as she lay there languidly sleepy, her stream of consciousness had been unedited. Honest.

He scratched his chin and wondered for a moment if he'd liked it. *Babe.* Yes, he liked it.

"Girlfriend, eh?" Nick was not letting that go. Typical.

"Just drive, preferably somewhere where no one will see us. I don't want to be recognized with you."

"Relax. People might think I'm just another suit."

Jackson didn't answer, instead stared ahead at the road.

"Are you gonna pretend you don't know why I came?"

Nick asked the moment they cleared town. Twenty minutes and he pulled off to the side of an empty field. Then he got out of the car and waited. After a moment, Jackson got the message and followed suit.

"I'm sure you got a reason, just not sure I know what it is." The comeback felt hollow; after all, they both knew why he'd come. Jackson kicked at a rock and it flew several yards into a dusty meadow.

"It's time, Jacks. Time you came home. I know you said you were coming after the PRCAs, but things are heating up. I need you now. The wildlife commission wants to cull the migrating herds. They're sending in a team. It's a mess, and if we can't show a program, they will get rid of the nonindigenous colors. You're out of time."

Jackson kicked another rock, sending this one clear over a broken picket fence. "Look, I already agreed to come for a bit to help you sort out the mustangs." He knelt and reached for another rock, hefting it from hand to hand and avoiding eye contact with Nick. It didn't make sense. The wildlife commission was in the Hartmann pocket. Something else was going on. Why was Nick really there?

"Don't you think that this petulant child act is getting a little old?" For the first time since Jackson could remember, Nick's voice was rising, aggravation setting in. "Do you even know how many people would give their eyeteeth to have your privilege?"

"Let them have it then. Let's donate my share of the estate right now." He flung the rock far afield and kicked up another pile of dust.

Nick let out a frustrated exhale and aimed his own kick at a fair size rock. "I don't think you mean that."

Jackson stared at the field cloaked in colors of the early-morning sun. "I meant it. I mean it. I'll come and help. I owe you for enabling me to find my way, but I'm not coming back. Not really."

Nick ran a hand across his chin. "That's not why I came."

There was something about his voice, something a little too calm.

Jackson sat back against the hood of the Lexus, the warm heat of the engine a nice offset to the cool early morning mist.

"It's Mia."

Two words. Amazing how your perspective could change in just two words.

Mia was Jackson's favorite. The younger of their twin stepsisters, the one who had always lived to please.

"What about her?" he asked, voice gruff with emotion.

Nick rounded the car and leaned next to him on the hood. "She is not good." The pronouncement distinct and effective.

Jackson pressed his eyes shut. He could see her. See every bit of her, defiant, proud, adorable. Hurting. "She's strong. She's smart. Better off without me, that's for sure." Jackson picked at a cuticle, intent on the task at hand.

"Well, your little sister found a father figure after all. Scott is ten miles of bad road and has left quite the mess of our little sis."

With an intensity that surprised him, Jackson pounded

the hood of the car, marveling at the dent his fist left. "Scott? That scumbag? He cheated on her after only four years of marriage? So you can call me the minute you get a little shade from the commissioner but not when our sister gets her heart broken by the scum of the earth?"

He stood and kicked the tire, recoiling at the sharp pain that resulted.

"A millionaire is not exactly the type you can boss around, in case you hadn't noticed. And Austin supported the match." Both men quieted at the mention of their late brother. Eighteen months after Austin and his wife died in a helicopter accident, he still found ways to manipulate and ruin the family. Austin supporting the match should have been warning enough that it was a bad idea.

"Probably got a payoff," Jackson mumbled under his breath. That was the problem with cutting your ties and ignoring your roots. Sometimes it ended in a root canal. Horrifically painful with messy follow-up.

"What's done is done. Scott's family have kept first steps of the divorce out of the press, and before you know it, Mia will be better off. But she's hurting, Jacks. Anyway, Scott's gone, left her for another woman or series of women… To be honest, I'm not sure why he left."

"Why doesn't matter. The why never matters."

"Amelia—Mia…she's okay. I mean she's a robot, doesn't like *anyone* anymore, but other than that, she's okay."

"We're all damaged." Jackson looked at the horizon stonily and wondered about Hannah. What was her baggage? Why would a woman like her agree to expiration dating? Surely she deserved more.

They didn't say anything. Instead, Jackson straightened, his correct posture the picture of professionalism.

"I'm trying. Trying to glue it back together. Help me?" Nick asked, his voice earnest.

"You don't need my help." Jackson said the words all the while wishing they weren't true. "Look, I got a contract." Then he softened. "I already gave notice though. I'm through with the circuits after the PRCA. Then I'll come home."

The PRCA was the win that would make a difference. The ungettable get for his father, who'd rode rodeo but never won the PRCA. This ride was the one that would make a difference for Brad Hill.

"And you will stay?" Nick persisted.

"It's never enough for you, one win? Never enough."

"I don't consider this a win," Nick corrected. "It's the only way forward. We have to heal together."

"I can't promise you anything." Despite himself, his thoughts flickered to the redhead left in bed. He couldn't promise her anything either. Even if he wanted to. Sometimes, leaving was a kindness. But maybe, just maybe, if he confronted his demons, he could keep her. It just might be worth it.

"Just do your best, Jacks. Just do your best."

Jackson nodded, swallowing the feeling he'd harbored for ten years. Sadly, where his family was concerned, his best was never going to be enough.

Ten

On the Road Again

"Third out of the gate tonight is Brad Hill, ladies and gentlemen. On a winning streak of four wins, Brad has set two records on the Montana circuit. He's paired tonight on Viper, so be prepared for a cinematic showdown." The announcer's voice blared through the stadium, but Hannah tuned out the other competitors' bios.

"Worst part of my night," she muttered under her breath.

"If you hate the rodeo so much, why do you come?" Mikey accused.

"Never said I hated the rodeo," she said defensively, all the while thinking to herself that the man had a point.

"Label on that beer bottle might suggest otherwise,"

Rodney shot back. He'd noticed she'd picked it off in a nervous tic.

Rodney? She was starting to think maybe he'd done her a kindness by abandoning Amy at the first sign of pregnancy. He was dismissive. And according to her mother, he was also undeniably her father, so that was just great. True, she hadn't yet told him. The minute she told him, it was likely going to be over, and she didn't want to waste one moment of time with Brad. She didn't have many of them left. For the first time ever, she felt like she belonged to someone. With someone. Maybe it wasn't the man she'd thought she'd get to know in Montana, but being with Brad was a game changer. She belonged.

Brad Hill was the bright spot in her day. And she was still four weeks away from the expiration date, so there was time enough to fully profit from their arrangement. Even if the sense of belonging was surely fleeting, she'd take it while it lasted.

"Are you riding tonight?" she asked Mikey.

The kid blushed. "Yeah, I'm supposed to go on fifth, but I don't need to suit up until Brad's done. They don't want to clog up the chute."

"Good luck." She squeezed his leg and the young guy pinked at the touch.

"Thanks," he mumbled. "Of course, I'm right in the same circuit as Brad, so my chances are pretty much zero."

"Still not too sure I understand why you cowboys like the rodeo so much."

"I reckon I like it the same reason Brad does."

His answer piqued her interest in a way no other could

have. It was the one no-go zone in their expiration dating. She never asked the questions she wanted most to resolve. *Why do you ride rodeo? Why do you never speak about your family? Have you ever had a real girlfriend?*

Mikey stared at his feet then let out a reluctant smile. "You know what they call July?"

She shook her head. She didn't know.

"Cowboy Christmas. So many rodeos in July, it puts tons of prize money up for grabs. Nampa, Salinas. Cheyenne. Salt Lake."

"You're listing them like I haven't been in the van for a month driving and burning the midnight oil to watch you lot ride."

The arena smelled like hot dogs and beer and sweat, and manure and excitement and fear. But everything fell away the minute Brad came out of the chute.

There was no denying it. There was something beautiful about watching him ride. Brad didn't look scared or concerned or frenetic. He concentrated, sure, but there was no mistaking that dimple she could see even at fifty yards. As Hannah watched, the sound slipped away. The people, crowds, slipped away. It was only her watching him as he did what he loved.

Celebrating another gold buckle wasn't the worst way to spend an evening. She waited by his truck. "Hi, handsome," she whispered.

"Hi yourself, beautiful." He threw the rope he was shouldering into the flatbed of the truck and pulled her onto the cock of his hip. He smelled like shower gel, but she closed her eyes to absorb the deeper, familiar scent she'd become addicted to. Tannins, oils from the ropes and leather and horse melded with the deep earthy musk of cedar and amber wood.

"You smell divine," she murmured into his chest.

He growled in response. "There's an area of you I'd like to get a little closer to," he promised, dipping his head to feast on her neck.

She wondered briefly if he could feel her racing pulse beneath his tongue as he tasted her from chin to collarbone with a practiced methodology.

"Not here." She stopped him.

"Is this about Rodney again?" he grumbled. It wasn't as though she'd mentioned her trepidation around Rodney, but it was undeniable. PDAs were not a possibility around her dad.

"It's just not professional," she explained, instantly regretting any protest that separated her neck from his lips.

"No, you have a good point. I don't want any of the other cowboys to get any ideas." In four weeks, they had managed to keep their trysts a total secret.

"Yes, you're right. Let's go have a celebratory drink then?" She pasted on a practiced smile and spun.

He grabbed her hand. "Actually, I did have a little something for you."

The admission surprised her. "We're only expiration dating..." she started. "Didn't realize you celebrated anniversaries or... Why did you even get me anything?" The confusion sank in as she stood paralyzed with curiosity.

The box he fished out of the driver's-side door was slim but long. Too long to be jewelry; a revelation that both disappointed yet reassured her.

"Just something I thought you'd like." He shrugged as he handed it over to her. "And if it's all the same to you, I'd like to take you somewhere tonight. Not too far, but it's a bit of a drive." He made the request quietly, which fascinated her.

"Are you blushing?" she teased, grateful for the opportunity to shift focus back on her hunky expiration boyfriend.

"It's hot," he protested. "You gonna open it or what?"

The box was heavy. Heavier than she'd expected. She opened it then snapped the lid shut. Her throat felt thick with emotion.

"You hate it."

He was beside her again; standing so close, she could feel his nervousness. He was picking at his thumb again, and she swatted it away. She couldn't speak. It was the nicest gift anyone had ever gotten her. A rose-gold-plated stethoscope. It was top-of-the-line. A 3M Littmann Classic. With an engraving. *Tell me where it hurts*.

"I love it."

When he reached for her, she didn't move. Couldn't move. She knew, at that moment, she was falling for him. Hard. He knew her. Better than anyone. And the part of her heart he'd stolen was exactly where it was going to hurt a month from now.

When he kissed her, she felt it reverberate in her chest. Felt it in her toes. In every part of her body.

"I gotta tell you something," he admitted. "Can we just skip the party tonight?"

"I'd love to." She reached for the truck door and climbed in. Bring on the pain.

Brad was quiet as he drove. When he passed the turn-off for their motel, she didn't speak. She just pointed to their exit in the rearview mirror.

"I know, but I gotta tell you something." It was the second time he'd said it, but instead of offering a revelation, he gripped the wheel harder. It was impossible not to notice how white the tips of his fingers were against the leather of the steering wheel.

"It's not like we have an audience," she said.

When he didn't respond, instead of pressing her question, she settled back into the passenger seat. His hand snaked over, adding a pleasant pressure to her leg. She smiled, covering it with her own. "No rush, I can wait."

Studying his profile, she noticed him swallow again.

"Do you trust me?" he probed.

Resisting the urge to answer right away, she just squeezed his hand. "Where are you taking me, Brad?"

"Big Sky is just shy of an hour from Bozeman, and we're already riding west. Twenty minutes and we'll get there."

She stared at his fingers, renewing their tight clench on the steering wheel.

"We're going to Bozeman?" She smiled. Bozeman was cool. Not exactly where she thought she'd be spending her evening, but still, not bad.

"I want you to know me."

He made the statement without looking at her, but it sliced through her. This time, it was he who squeezed her hand. She wanted to know him too. To belong, for real.

With her free hand, she opened the slim box again and took out the stethoscope. It was amazing. She re-read the inscription. *Tell me where it hurts.*

"You shouldn't have spent all your money on this. I mean I get them at the hospital." She was both incredibly touched and self-conscious about the gift.

"I didn't."

"Didn't?" she pressed. The truck had hit downtown Bozeman, and she was momentarily distracted by the lights. He slowed in front of the Kimpton Armory, an imposing heritage building renovated to a modern, sleek, boutique hotel.

He rolled down the passenger window and put the truck in Neutral, grinning at the valet as he tossed a set of keys across her lap.

"I didn't spend all my money." He winked at her.

With the chivalry of an old-school cowboy, Brad was at her door, opening it and extending a hand to help her step down.

"I didn't pack a bag or anything," she had the presence of mind to say.

"Taken care of," he assured her. "The valet will arrange to have our bags brought to the suite."

The few steps up to the lobby were exciting. Was he letting his guard down?

At the top of the steps, he stopped, spinning to face her. "I can kiss you here, right? We don't know anyone." Without waiting for an answer, he pressed a kiss, searing hot, onto her inexpectant lips.

Hannah moaned, embarrassed at the reaction, but his expert kisses had her head spinning.

"If you're gonna make sounds like that, I'll never be able to stop. And even if we don't know these people, it might be a bad idea to put on this kinda show for the adoring public."

The lobby was resplendent. Soaring high ceilings and marble floors polished to an impossible shine. Staff and bellboys attending high marble-topped counters smiled.

"Fancy a bite to eat before we check in?" Brad asked, his face twitching. The twitch was new, a quick tightening of his jaw that was impossible to ignore.

Hannah smiled. "As you like."

Instead of pulling off into the lobby bar, he ushered her toward the elevators at the back. A terse nod from a bellboy and a key was swiped at the elevator that led to a rooftop restaurant. Brad thanked him and they stepped into the mirrored elevator.

No sooner did the doors close than he crushed her against him. He kissed her so thoroughly, a second groan escaped, which served only to fuel him forward. His hands roamed her body with a calculated possession she found both primitive and hot as hell. A muscled grip locked onto her hips, lifting her to lean on the polished handrail of the elevator. She opened her eyes and was struck by the 360-degree view of his passion. The mirrored interior offered her an out-of-body experience to his ardor.

His hands pushed under her skirt, fingers exploring. Hannah widened her stance, allowing him unfettered access.

"If we weren't in an elevator right now..." he breathed into her hair.

Hannah tilted her chin back, leaning her head against the mirrored wall. She stared up, watching his muscled shoulders hunch as he touched her. Then she closed her eyes and lost herself in his touch.

All too soon, the ride was over. He pulled away from her as the ding alerted them to the doors opening.

Brad walked her toward an available table, seating them with utter confidence. It was a different side to him, so at ease in a distinct setting.

"It's beautiful up here," Hannah proclaimed, despite the mixed feelings running rampant. She cared about Brad too much. He wasn't supposed to be the family she needed.

"Yep. Not that I get to Bozeman much these days." He was staring off into the distance. Here, but not with her.

The waitress arrived; a young, flirty woman slim enough to make Hannah put a protective hand on her own muffin top, offering to get them drinks.

"The cocktail of the day is an old-fashioned, garnished with candied ginger."

"I'll have that," Hannah breathed, glad to avoid consulting an extensive drink menu.

"Two," Brad said. His decision was curt and dismissed more than the waitress. Surely, his abrupt order would also quiet any flirty ideas she might harbor. "Or did you want a mint julep?"

"Not that I'm complaining about my *Pretty Woman* moment, but do you think you might tell me what's going on?" If she'd learned one thing in med school, it was the importance of having the guts to ask the tough questions.

"Doesn't a guy have a right to take his girlfriend away for a surprise night out on the town?" He grinned at her with an infuriating attractiveness.

"Brad. Seriously. You said you wanted to tell me

something. You brought me here, out of the blue, to what I can only assume is a wildly expensive restaurant, in a wildly expensive hotel, where I'm guessing we're spending the night, so what is it?"

He took his hat off. It wasn't a good sign when he took his hat off. But he didn't put it on the table. Instead he spun it around, staring at it intently.

"I guess I just want you to know me."

"I do know you, Brad. Six weeks and spending every night together. I know you."

Then he put his hat down. He leaned forward and pressed both hands into the tabletop.

"To start, my name isn't Brad."

He watched her carefully after the confession. Watched as she wore her perfect mask, her smile frozen in place, her hair curling around her jaw. Her face was blank, the kind of face a surgeon used when delivering bad news. Was that it? Was she preparing bad news for him?

"What is it then? Your name? You can follow it with an explanation." Her voice was quiet and he pressed forward to hear better.

"My name is Jackson." That was the easy part. "Jackson Hartmann," he added, waiting for the ball to drop.

You didn't come to Bozeman, Montana, without knowing exactly who the Hartmann family was. It was also why he hadn't needed to give a name to reception or to the hostess to get the best table at the rooftop restaurant. Even in rodeo gear, in Bozeman, his face was unmistakable. That was why he didn't compete in Bozeman. He didn't want to blur the lines of Brad Hill and

Jackson Hartmann. Lines that were becoming more and more difficult to differentiate.

"As in Hartmann Homestead?" she clarified. "As in the Hartmann wing of Bozeman Memorial?"

"Pretty sure we sponsor the entire hospital these days."

He watched her. Watched her watching him. Her face was pale, the freckles standing out once again.

"Why? Why would you lie? To me?" She reached for the napkin and twisted it more with disappointment than anger. She wound it into an impossibly tight knot then twisted it in the opposite direction.

"This was a mistake. I shouldn't have told you here, shouldn't have told you like this." The ball of nerves in his stomach was on fire. Was he pushing too much? Was it crazy to fight for everything he'd always been afraid to want? Was it the prospect of going back home? The prospect of confronting Nick and Rose that also made him confront a void in himself? *No. Not that.*

"I think your mistake was not being honest from the beginning." But her voice was quiet. That wasn't the issue, and he was relieved by the assumptions he drew from her feeble protest. She'd known him as Brad before they were dating. It wasn't a *new* lie. He hoped that made it better.

"I told you that my dad left. I was honest with you. More honest than I've ever been with anyone. You have to know that." This was the hard part, the part he'd been hoping to avoid with her stupid expiration dating.

"Why are you coming clean now? Why not keep lying to me if I'm just some woman you're expiration dating?"

"You're not 'some woman,' and I think you know

it. And I think you also know this is more than expiration dating, even if that's all it can ever be." Mercifully, the waitress arrived with two old-fashioneds and he reached for his glass, dosing his regret with alcohol, a time-proven method for coping.

She reached for her glass but didn't sip. Instead, she pulled off the candied ginger then dropped it into the glass, watching with fascination as it sank.

"I feel really mad at you." Her voice was quiet, but in the low, scratchy tone, it was almost scarier.

"I'm mad at me too." Sometimes the easiest way out was the truth, not that he had learned that from his father.

She didn't answer, just took a deep sip of her drink. "Why Brad Hill?"

He picked his hat up again and spun it around like a fidget spinner for a grown man.

The air was cooler on the roof, and he saw her shiver. "Can I give you my coat?" he asked. It was easier asking the question than answering one.

"Why Brad Hill?" she repeated, leveling her gaze.

"I don't know, Hannah. Don't you ever just want to be someone else for a minute, or decade, or forever?"

To hate your own heritage was a burden. A heavy one he'd been shouldering for the better part of fifteen years. How had Nick done it? Moved on from the nightmare and found—no, *made*—a home? He swallowed. It was easier being Brad. But, not for the first time, he considered the mantra he repeated preride. *If it isn't hard, it isn't worth it.* And if anyone was worth it, it was Hannah.

Her gaze fell, and she half whispered, "Yeah. I get

wanting to hide who you are." Then her eyes made contact again, widening in sympathy. So she did get it.

"I promise not to hide anything more from you. At least, not for the next three and a half weeks." It was easier to accept the challenge on an expiration basis. The deadline gave him an out. If DNA was any measure, he was as much his father as he was Nick, and he couldn't bear the thought of being wrong about who he was. The PRCA championship was never more important.

As he voiced the timeline allowed, he regretted it. He knew with a certainty he hadn't yet experienced that he couldn't quit her. Didn't want to quit her. But he'd deal with quitting when the time came.

His grin provoked one of hers and his relief was palpable.

"So now that it's all out there, I think we can finish this with some room service in the presidential suite?"

She picked up her glass in mock cheers and drained it, all the while keeping eye contact. Then Boston winked.

"Put it on the room," he instructed the server as they walked toward the elevator. But instead of turning to press the brass down button, he led her past the hallway, fishing a key from his pocket.

"The valet," he explained sheepishly.

His fingers were cold. He was nervous. He'd never been with a woman as himself; he'd always had the character of Brad Hill to lean on. The rodeo rider. The horse whisperer. But tonight? With her? All he had to offer was himself.

He opened the doors to the presidential suite, but it was more than that. It was a door to what was possible, a portal back to where he'd come from. But with her, it seemed more tenable, positive even. Maybe, just maybe, in this circumstance right now, he *wanted* to be a Hartmann. With her, he wanted to be Jackson.

He watched Hannah carefully as she took in the room. It was opulent. The four-poster was a California king bedecked with Egyptian linen and velvet throws. The gas fireplace was lit, and in front of it was a table with a tray of charcuterie, and two champagne flutes beside a bucket with the chilling Prosecco. Ornate lamps with polished brass stems and black linen shades scattered the room, all alight and issuing a soft glow. Whoever designed the space was clearly a fan of indirect lighting.

But he wasn't watching any of that. He was watching her. And she, him.

She brought a hand to her shoulder. She pushed the strap of her sundress away then repeated the same action to the other shoulder. The dress pooled at her waist and, with a shimmy, she stepped out of it.

No fancy lingerie this time. She wore a cotton bra and underwear that didn't match. She didn't fold her arms over her body; instead she pressed her shoulders back and shook her head so that her hair fell around her.

"Do you like the room?" he joked, his mouth suddenly dry. He was impressed that he'd managed to speak in the face of her explicit nudity.

"I like you, Jackson." The way she said his name, like she savored the sound of it and was ready for a more satisfying second course… He swallowed.

He kicked off his boots and unbuttoned his shirt. He had thought there was nothing more attractive than Hannah Bean standing naked before him, but there was. It was Hannah Bean standing naked before him and calling him Jackson.

He kissed her without ceremony, deliberate and thorough. He cradled her face. Kissed the tip of her nose. Her forehead. Each cheek.

But it was more than a kiss. It was a prayer. An absolution. A quiet forgiveness asked and answered. And, God, it felt good. He sank to his knees and pressed his face into her, inhaling until she filled every sense he had. Slipping a thumb into the elastic of her panties, he rid her of the last scraps of modesty, but she didn't move. Just stood, fingers twisted in his hair. Tugging him forward, not that he needed convincing.

For as long as he could remember, he'd liked women. Loved women. Liked to love women. But this one? There was something addictive about her. His hands descended and his fingers traced the curves of her legs. Soft, dimpled flesh so feminine he could barely stand it. She was as soft as he was hard, and he was very hard indeed.

He felt the sharp pain in his scalp as she tugged him up, but he refused to abandon his current course, preferring to taste her more thoroughly than had been done as of yet.

"I love the way you smell," he paused long enough to say.

She took a step back, sinking onto the bed. "Stop it, you're being ridiculous." She pushed him away, but he caught her wrist and pressed a kiss to the base of her hand.

"Nothing ridiculous about it. If I die right now, I die happy."

She laughed, but it was a soft laugh. The kind of laugh you issue when you don't want to cry.

"Your body is perfect," he said, voice heavy with reverence. He was blabbering, repeating the same nonsense time and time again. But he couldn't stop. His train of kisses continued, interrupted only by her tugging on his belt and relieving him of his jeans.

Naked, he joined her, determined to take his time. To use his body to say all the things he couldn't. All the things he wasn't ready to say.

"What's taking so long, cowboy?"

Despite his good intentions, he couldn't wait any longer. He covered her body with his, entering her in one thrust while taking her mouth with a desperation that matched his hips. He traced the curve of her waist to her hip and stroked her with a punishingly slow tempo.

"Stop teasing me." She bucked her hips up and caught his bottom lip between her teeth.

"Careful, Boston." He pulled away, still sunk to the hilt in her warmth.

She bucked again and he redoubled his efforts.

When she climaxed around him, he allowed himself to follow.

Truth was, he'd follow her anywhere.

Eleven

Benefits and Bad News

Room service was one of everything on the breakfast menu. Enough food to feed the entire floor, except in their case the entire floor was occupied by their suite, and they were the only two in it.

"It's too much," Hannah protested, all the while thinking it wasn't enough. Her time with him wasn't going to be enough.

"It's always a bad idea to order food when you're hungry," Jackson growled. "And right now, I'm starving."

Ignoring the breakfast, he traced once again the curve of her hip and she willed herself every ounce of confidence she possessed to lie back on their bed, the 10:00 a.m. sunshine offering little in the way of modesty.

He explored her with the lazy thoroughness that only Sunday morning could offer. His fingertips felt light on her skin yet insistent on their path.

"Haven't you had enough of me yet?" she breathed as his roaming exploration brought his touch to the apex of her thighs. He didn't answer, just dipped one finger inside her, finding her as ready for him as she had been all night. All week. All the time.

She reached for him and he grinned at her, pushing away her hand. "I just want to touch you. I don't want any distractions. I want to enjoy this, enjoy you…" He kissed her hip bone as his fingers flexed inside her.

Again and again, he circled until she shook beneath him. Her whole body was tight with anticipation, wound up by his expert ministrations. Jackson played her body like an instrument he'd spent his life studying.

Her finish was as shattering as ever; an explosion of emotion and gratification, tampered by guilt. Jackson had come clean, but she? She was still hiding a truth central to her being.

He pressed a kiss onto her forehead and waved away her renewed effort to touch him.

"Just for you," he repeated, following it up with a second kiss. Firm and final.

"What are we gonna do today?" Hannah reached for a buttery croissant, breaking off the flaky tip and immediately embarrassed at the ensuing crumbs scattering the bed. At least the mess kept her mind off the naked man lying, distracted, beside her.

His fingers rested under the curve of her breast and she lightly smacked his hand before it could find purchase.

"I told you I was hungry." He bent his neck and bit into the soft skin of her hip.

Swiping him away with the croissant, scattering more crumbs with the action, she laughed. "I actually think you owe me…" she started.

"That is precisely my point. And I've got a few detailed ideas as to how I can make it up to you."

"Jackson," she threatened, picking up a still-warm breakfast roll and lobbing it in his direction.

He stilled, not bothering with razor-sharp reflexes that could have deflected the pastry. "I forgot. For a minute, I forgot that you knew."

"You thought a night of lovemaking would make me forget? Was that your plan then?" She ran a hand through her hair, pulling her bangs off her face to tuck behind her ear.

"No. I didn't think that."

She swallowed the rest of her croissant and studied him. His eyes were ringed and heavy from lack of sleep; she was perhaps to blame for that. His lips were drawn and gone was that dimple she so cherished. She reached for another roll, a brioche of all things, and chucked it at him. This one, he caught.

"I'm glad you know."

"You said your dad left." She put it out there, gave him the space to tell her more. There were no drinks, no twilight magic or heady sexual tension to distract them. Just her and him. "Why don't you tell me more? You know, actually *talk* to me."

Jackson pulled himself up onto his arms and reached for a pillow to stuff behind him. "What? You want my 'poor little rich boy' story? That my mom died and my dad remarried? You want to know that my own father didn't pick us? That he had a whole other family no one knew about?

"Yeah. That's right. There was another woman. There was always another woman. But Rachel—her name was Rachel—was different. One day Bart just up and left, choosing to live with them, this other family, and he was gone seven years. Didn't even send a card. I don't know anything about them, apart from her name. None of us do. All I know is they lived in Colorado, with *my* father… I wasn't sad, not for me, but the twins? Nick? Austin?" Despite himself, his voice cracked.

She didn't say anything, just reached out, and took his hand. The movement was simple, but anchored him. He wanted her to know more. Know him.

"Or do you want to hear about how my grandparents and everybody always fought about money like it had the superpower that made us all impervious to real human problems? How my grandparents blamed us for our dad leaving, and my stepmom was desperate with grief and finding herself responsible for raising kids that weren't hers? How maybe, just maybe, everyone had a point? About the money? About dad leaving? Is it so hard to understand why I didn't want to be in that world? Why wouldn't I leave that toxicity behind?"

"But…you have siblings. Your mom didn't leave, she died. I mean…surely it wasn't all toxic?" Her voice was small; she kept it quiet on purpose, almost worried that speaking forcefully might scare him away from being open.

Jackson fidgeted again on the bed then swung his legs off the side and turned his back to her. "I'm getting coffee." He pointed to the room service cart that had magically arrived outside their door that morning. "You want one?"

"Yeah. I'll take it with a side of *tell me about your mother*." Maybe if she hammered him with prompts, it would work.

Her sarcasm did elicit a laugh, not to mention the added benefit of inciting a bedside delivery of a luke-warm latte. But she thirsted for something a little different. Knowledge.

"You're not gonna let this go, are you?"

"Doing one of those lawyer tricks where you only ask questions you already know the answer to?" She smiled and shook her head in a predictable no.

"I had two big brothers who fought constantly in some sort of competitive one-upmanship I couldn't even imagine being a part of. It's like they thought if they were good enough, my dad would come back. Then there's the twins, younger than me and clever as can be. Mia was my favorite, but the poor girl never had a chance. My stepmom, Josephine, locked herself away for a year after dad left, not quite mother of the year for eight-year-old twin girls."

He'd said earlier his sisters were two years his junior. That would have made him just a kid when his dad had left his family to start another one. "Not to mention a ten-year-old?" Hannah pressed, unable to not think about what this must have meant for Jackson, eyes sting-ing with unspent tears. She could imagine it. Jackson, cute as a button, quite likely, trying to make sense of his dad disappearing from one day to the next. Trying to make sense of a mom who'd checked out, and two younger sisters forcing him to grow up fast.

He wasn't looking at her. It was probably easier that way and she just nodded so as not to interrupt his train of thought.

"I always loved horses. Mia too. When my dad came back, he bought her a beautiful horse, and I taught her how to ride it."

"So you always were a horse whisper."

His smile was encouraging. At least there was a bright spot in his otherwise depressing childhood.

He shrugged. "When dad returned, desperate to save the marriage and get things back in line, I was seventeen and didn't feel all right about his reinsertion into our lives. How could Josephine, or any of us, trust him coming back? We had a terrible fight. I wanted to expand our cattle operation. Well, change it. Wanted to breed mustangs, stallions. I guess you *could* say I was a horse whisper. As much as one could be at seventeen."

She sipped her coffee, grateful that her hands had something to do.

Jackson's face darkened. "Well, dear old dad didn't like that. Didn't like anyone telling him what to do. 'You can't fight your destiny, Jackson.' Told me instead he reckoned that I always had a face for politics. Wanted me to shape my future to be a head of state or some other suit-wearing nightmare. When I disagreed, Mia defended me. Bragged about how I'd trained the perfect horse for her. Dad didn't like that much." Jackson paused, taking a breath. "He went and shot it dead."

Hannah wanted to cry. They weren't so different. Sure, she'd grown up poor, but they were both independent. Both a little wild. And both wildly disappointed by their families. For the first time, she couldn't help but wonder if Jackson longed for a family every bit as much as she did.

"I got on a stallion, one I'd corralled only a few weeks earlier and rode off. Bareback. Bart followed on another horse, one of the mustangs. Snake in the field scared the horse, who reared up and threw him. Bart died a week later, victim to the injuries of falling off a stallion made up of a half ton of muscle.

"We never did make things right. You can't fight who you are, and my father wasn't a good man."

"I'm sorry. That feels so…not enough. *I'm sorry?* Like those two words could bring you any kind of comfort or understanding. But it doesn't make them less true because… I am. Sorry."

"I don't know what to do now, Hannah. About Nick? Mia? She needs me. But I can't go home yet. I need to win, need to show my dad I'm enough. Better than him. A winner, and not because of his legacy. Because of me."

"Nick's your brother…" She said it as a statement rather than a question, sure of its accuracy.

Jackson nodded. "To be fair, we did work together." He took a sip of his coffee. "Look, I know I owe you an apology. A verbal apology."

Hannah flushed, remembering the physical one he'd made the night prior. It was the type to incite forgiveness. Perhaps even the type of apology that would incite more fights. If making up was that much fun, she didn't see the problem in a mild provocation from time to time.

"I don't need zero to hero. You don't have to get it all out right now." As much as she wanted him to, she still had secrets of her own, and if he came entirely clean, where did that leave her? As far from family as she'd started. Even more alone.

She reached for him, drawing him into a tight hug, and he obliged. Anything to avoid thinking about that night, and the one in eight chance he'd draw Mayhem.

Hannah could count on one hand the amount of times her heart had frozen. She could perfectly recall the few occasions her heart had jumped into her throat, robbing her of the ability to talk or move or act. Mostly in her youth, the episodes had involved her feral birth parent, but she'd long since disassociated from Amy's antics. Freezing up was a phase she'd hoped to have grown out of. In fact, in med school, she'd been renowned for her nerves of steel. But now? Now it was happening again. She was frozen. She was powerless. And she was utterly afraid.

"Get out there," Rodney yelled over his shoulder. With an agility that surprised her, he'd hopped the railings and was barging toward the crumpled body. Toward Jackson.

But Hannah? She couldn't move. She was frozen.

There was a medic. Hannah registered the litter, the hard board the paramedic team transferred Jackson onto.

"Come on." It was Mikey, tugging her arm. But she just stared.

"What's wrong with her?" she heard Will ask Mikey.

Robotically, she looked at her fingertips. The telltale bluish tinge colored the tips and betrayed the first signs of shock. Then her chest heaved of its own accord, a quick succession of rapid breaths. She pressed her eyes shut with the vain hope that perhaps, if she could blot out the accident, she'd recoup her senses. She'd regain control. But all her shut eyes provided was a backdrop for her brain to replay the hit.

Jackson had dismounted with an elegance that had secured him another gold buckle, oblivious to Carter's bull who'd charged out of his gate unannounced. A mechanical failure, Carter had proclaimed. The chute opening and Viper running full speed at an unsuspecting Jackson.

She'd seen it in slow motion. Unable to speak. Unable to call out. The arena watched in silence as he'd been rammed, his body writhing in the air. Then the crack on landing. It hadn't taken a doctor to know it was bad. But he'd rolled. Jackson had somehow leaned on his muscle memory to roll to the edge of the arena, narrowly avoiding a trampling.

Regardless, the damage was done. Adrenaline could take you far, but not far enough. Hannah was sure of only one thing: Jackson was hurt, and he was hurt badly.

"She rides with him. She's with us."

It was Rodney who insisted, and before she could protest, she was in the ambulance. It smelled like antiseptic and blood, an odor comforting only in its familiarity. Hannah reached for Jackson's hand.

"Boston," Jackson murmured, eyes opening a crack. His fingers squeezed on hers, a good sign.

Another good sign, his optic nerve hadn't been damaged by the impact. "I'm here," she promised, bobbing her head.

"Don't look so worried." He offered up a pained grin. *Ha.* As if she could be anything but terrified.

"You trying to tell me what to do again?" She managed a grin of her own. *Don't cry.*

"Move, miss." The paramedic was cutting open Jackson's shirt, nudging her toward his head. Just as well. She moved an open palm to cup his cheek.

"I'm right here," she told him, holding back a wave of emotion.

His face was battered. She had a bird's-eye view of his back, black-and-blue with hoof marks, and bruising. A nasty purple was spreading across his abdomen.

"He's okay, miss. He's going to be okay," the kind paramedic assured her. But Hannah was a doctor.

"You can't know that. You can't know that until they do tests." Her voice rose in tone, each accusation more strangled than the last.

"Boston, you worry too much," Jackson added, his shallow breaths doing little to reassure her.

"Three minutes out," the paramedic said into the handheld.

The news, offered after three hours of tests and several labs, was good, he supposed. A cracked spine, but not broken.

"You're a lucky man," the doctor reminded Jackson.

It was hard to feel lucky with a neck brace and more than one IV tube attached to his arm. Hannah was there; she was with them every step of the way. It had been a challenge to hold her back from questioning and second-guessing every piece of medical advice and information that had been offered.

"How long till I'm back?" His right arm was unencumbered and he lifted it to trace his fingers along the hard plastic of the neck brace then up to his hair, which he tousled. At least his hair wasn't broken. He smelled like dried blood, but none of the wounds was too deep. He was lucky, he reminded himself again.

"I expect you'll be able to walk out of here in short order," the doctor confirmed with a smile.

"Tell him," Hannah threatened. Her voice was low and gruff. The kind of voice that was heavier after hours spent crying.

"The fractures will heal—" the doctor said as he picked up the pace at which he tapped his pen against a plastic clipboard.

"If you don't ride anymore," Hannah interjected. "You *can't* ride anymore. Not the bulls. Baby, it's over."

The baby moniker evoked a startled breath from Rodney, who had been ever present since arriving directly behind the ambulance. "Let's not make any rash statements," he said. "He's already got enough points for the PRCA championships even if he doesn't ride for two weeks. What do you say, Doc, is there one ride left in him?"

Rodney's voice took on the slick salesmanship she'd seen him wield time and time again. She wanted to love him. She wanted to think he was a great guy, worthy of being her dad, but right now? She watched him try to sell another bull ride to her incapacitated boyfriend, and vitriolic hate roiled in her stomach. In an extreme conflict of loyalty, she swallowed it back and smiled at them both.

"Doc?" It was Jackson who pressed for more clarity.

"Your spine's not in good shape. Sorry to say, but your girlfriend is right. You are a lucky man. I've seen similar accidents go other ways, and I can tell you another bad fall and that fissure will be a clean break."

"Clean break?"

"Paralysis. Irreversible." The doctor nodded.

"No riding." Hannah was shaking her head and bringing her fingers to her eyes, rubbing their swollen lids.

"But his spine is in good shape. And he *could* be fine. It's only a problem if he falls, that's my understanding, right?" Rodney pressed.

"It would be inadvisable for him to compete in a professional rodeo at this time, if ever. That's my medical opinion, but you're welcome to find another." The doctor scanned the tense faces in the room then reached into his pocket to retrieve a buzzing pager.

Rodney fumed and reached for his tin of tobacco, slipping another bud under his lip.

"Silver lining, Rod. I *am* okay." Jackson smiled.

"You certainly are," Hannah reminded him. Momentarily appeased by the current resolution, her smile widened. "I'm going to stop by the cafeteria, see if there isn't something to eat. I'll bring you guys something back. Any requests?"

"Your pleasure is my pleasure," Jackson said as he winked at her. Even from the hospital bed, it felt good teasing her.

Rodney and Jackson watched as a faint blush spread on her cheeks. "Whatever." She rolled her eyes and exited.

Alone with his manager, Jackson gave himself a quick minute to take it all in, going through an inventory of the aches and pains. Truth was, he felt pretty darn good, but wiggling his toes and seeing them move was definitely reassuring.

Beside his bed, Rodney paced. His boots clicked on the aged linoleum of the hospital floor and Jackson questioned for a quick moment why they hadn't upgraded to a private suite.

"You don't get it, kid, which shouldn't surprise me. If you don't ride in the PRCAs, you're in breach of contract. And speaking of fancy contracts, you'll likely have to send back the advance. Your girlfriend here might not think it's so funny when she doesn't see another payday, because I don't need to remind you, the payday is attached to your competition in the PRCAs. The cowboys ride as long as they are able. Are you able or not? Are you a cowboy or not? What do you say, kid? You gonna let your family down?"

Jackson sat up in bed. There was no denying it. Rodney was flawed. Very flawed. But Jackson had leaned on him at seventeen as a confused kid with nowhere else to go. Rodney hadn't hesitated to offer him the back of his truck, not to mention a job he'd loved that had given him purpose.

"We're family again, eh? That's your pitch?" Truth was, family wasn't going to be the argument that got him on the back of a bucking bull, found family or not.

"I know it hasn't always been easy between us. But you're magic on the back of a bull. Heck, even this injury only happened because you were charged. By all accounts that won't happen again." Jackson had his doubts about this too. Carter was likely responsible. It made sense.

"Words are pretty cheap, Rod. They certainly will feel hollow if I fall."

"*If you fall*. Like, what are the chances? You've finished thirty rides in the past two months. You've fallen nine times. I mean them's single digits."

"It's easy for you. You're not the one risking anything."

Rodney stopped his pacing and stared at Jackson. Then he did something that surprised Jacks. He took his hat off and held it against his chest.

"If you do this, I'll never ask another thing of you. We call it quits after the PRCAs, and you won't owe me nothing. Nothing, after all I've done for you. I swear it. I'm asking you for eight seconds."

He was a salesman. And, for a minute, Jackson considered his request.

"Is this really how you want to leave rodeo?" Rodney pressed. "An injury that threw you on your ass? That's the end of Brad Hill, champion bull rider?"

Before he could stop himself, Jackson was shaking his head. "It's not the end."

Jackson wasn't ready to say goodbye to the rodeo. Wasn't ready to say goodbye to Brad Hill. He couldn't give up the chance to prove he was enough, even if it was only to a memory of a man he wouldn't ever face again. He would ride in the PRCAs and he would win. Because he wasn't ready to let go of the goal that had driven him away from the ranch and onto this path of accomplishment. But mostly, he wasn't ready to say goodbye to Hannah.

Twelve

Whistleblower

"What do you mean you're going to ride?" Hannah fumed. She trekked across their hotel room, feet soft against the lush carpet, pacing at a dizzying rhythm.

Jackson exhaled, counting to three. He'd been around enough angry females to know timing was everything. And Hannah? She was angry indeed.

"I think you're thinking about this all wrong."

"Oh, good." She ceased pacing and stared at him, eyes bright and hair wild on her shoulders. "Now you're going to risk your spinal column to make some point to someone who doesn't care about you. To someone who's dead."

Hannah had an answer for everything; it was one of the things he loved about her. Wait, no. He didn't love her.

They were expiration dating. He cleared his throat, willing himself to get his head back in the game. "I'm making the point to myself—"

She wagged a finger at him. "You're telling me now that you're going to ride the PRCA championships against medical advice to make a point? You have a chance to reunite with people who care about you." She stamped her foot to punctuate each syllable, pointing her finger for unnecessary emphasis. For a minute, he wondered if she was one of the people who cared about him.

His disclosure was hardly going to plan, but he had to admit he wasn't surprised at her displeasure. Butter could hardly melt in her mouth all morning. She had been over-the-top sweet and he knew why. She'd attempted to preempt his objection to pulling out of the circuit. To walk from his sponsorship. She'd tried to cut his opposition off at the legs, but this decision had to be his.

Thus far, Jackson had been adept at ignoring the little voice inside that echoed the doctor's concern. It was harder to ignore Hannah's worry. He pushed back the niggling thought that she had a point. Pushed back the feeling that maybe her worry was more important than his own manic need to win. But Rodney was right. If he and Hannah were meant to be, for the long haul, what was eight seconds? Couldn't he have both? Wouldn't he be a better man if he could put this ghost to bed? If he could win?

He cleared his throat again, running his hand through his hair and exhaling once more. "Against one doctor's advice. A doctor who has never seen me ride."

Hannah's eyes fell to the floor. With one remark, he'd

felled her. When she met his gaze again, her eyes were wet. "I'm a doctor. I've seen you ride. Does my opinion not matter?"

He closed the distance between them once again and pulled her into his chest. "Hannah, I need to make this decision for myself. I'm not the kind of man that does someone's bidding. I've never been that kind of man." He could still hear it. The echo of his dad's laugh as he repeated again and again that he and Nick were boys, not cowboys. That they'd never have the steel needed for rodeo. He could still hear the thud of Mia's horse as it hit the ground dead, followed by his father's insistence that real men weren't afraid to hurt. That real men won.

It was easier admitting the truth with her pressed against his chest. And then he felt the pound of a small fist just under the crux of his shoulder. "You can make this decision yourself as long as it's the right one."

Her insistence was confusing. He hadn't expected her to push so hard. To care so much. "You mean as long as it's the decision you want. I can make the decision as long as it's the outcome you agree with."

"I think you know what the difference is," she said. She was going to tell him. He could tell from the breathy feeling in her voice. She was gonna say three words that would change everything. But why?

"Don't. Don't even try to manipulate me. It won't work. I'm riding and there is nothing you can do but trust me. I've grown up riding. I won't lose this title or what it represents."

She choked. "What it represents?"

"Freedom. Can't you see that? I can't go back without it. I can't." He shook his head, finally having voiced the truth. He wanted to go home, but couldn't, not without the validation he needed to earn.

She pulled away with a ferocity that shocked him. "You have a name. You have a family that wants you to go home and you're too damn stubborn to see what a gift that is." She spun away from him, hair flying wild.

"Did Nick get to you?" He couldn't help it; that was the first place his mind went.

Hannah laughed, but the laugh was cold. Stoic. Detached. "Nick? You're so quick to see the worst in everyone else, never yourself. Did you ever think, Jackson, that you're a—" She choked on the words as he leaned in, a sick curiosity propelling him forward. Then she made the pronouncement with a final stab of her index. "A coward?"

He recoiled in vehemence. "Do you think a coward would risk everything, risk his legs, for honor?"

"Honor?" She laughed again. "Do you think an honorable man would turn his back on the kind of legacy that could change his family forever? The kind of legacy that could change him? Change you, Jackson? All I ever wanted was a family, stability and someone to fight for me. And you? You won't even fight for yourself. You'll burn it all down before you admit these people aren't bad. Before you admit the past is in the past."

Jackson walked to the marble fireplace at the edge of the penthouse suite he'd rented for his two-week recovery. Both his hands were hot against the smooth cool stone and he tightened his fingers around the ledge of the mantel, squeezing as though enough pressure could eke out a few tears from the stone. He had as much chance to eke out his own tears. He knew precisely what he had to do. But she was saying everything that he didn't want to hear. Reminding him of the arguments the devil on his shoulder had whispered this past year. She was right. He needed to let go. But eight seconds was hardly going to change everything. He'd move on as soon as the title was his.

Devil be gone, no one told Jackson Hartmann what to do.

"I'm sorry that you find me a man without honor. That's not the sort of man you want to be in a pact with, so I think it's for the best that we end this little expiration dating experiment now. That might relieve you of any misunderstanding that you have some say or opinion that matters."

He heard her sharp intake of breath behind him but didn't turn to look at her; instead he gripped the mantel, drawing strength from the impassivity of the structure. The impassivity of his position.

"I will compete in the PRCA championship. And I *will* win."

The air was thick with silence. He waited for her to argue. He waited for her to insist he was making a mistake, for her to fight and change his mind. How he wanted her to change his mind.

Instead, he heard her walk across the room, pick up her purse and leave.

When Jackson raised his head and looked in the mirror over the fireplace, his reflection shocked him. His cheek was wet with the lone track of an errant tear.

Hannah Bean gave up. On him. On her opinions. But he would ride in the PRCA championship, and she'd get paid. She was wrong. He could still be there for Nick.

This wasn't an either-or situation. He was a man of his word, and after the PRCAs, he'd go home. This buckle was all he'd needed. This buckle was for seventeen-year-old Jackson, and it was all within reach.

He stared at the door and pushed away the lump in his throat. It was all in his reach.

So why did he wish she'd stayed? Why did he wish she'd fought a little harder and changed his mind?

Hannah had seen it before. The look in an animal's eyes when it was cornered. When it knew there was only one way to go, one way out. Hannah felt it now. She *felt* the way those animals looked. Trapped. This. Now. She was here to do the last thing she wanted, but the only move she had.

"You have an appointment?" The receptionist spoke at her while staring through the lobby. The floors were polished marble and Hannah's thoughts were punctuated by the slapping of stilettos as well-dressed women scurried across the lobby.

Hannah pulled at the hem of her blouse. "Er, no, but it's important. I did call…" Her voice trailed off and she pushed her shoulders back, determined to sound more professional as she insisted, "I'm Hannah Bean. I'm here in regard to the Brad Hill contract?"

The receptionist was unfazed, and typed rapidly at her station, keys clicking as she nodded. "Mr. Jacobs can see you." The woman slid a plastic access card across the counter and Hannah picked it up with sweaty fingers.

"Take the elevator on the left. Mr. Jacobs is on the

eighteenth floor. Corporate reception will show you the way."

The receptionist returned her attention to the buzzing phones and Hannah, pushing her shoulders back again, made her way toward the elevator. The only choice she had.

The ride felt both punishingly long and unbearably short. It was impossible not to think about Jackson. What else could she think about? He was going to hate her, but this was what family did. They protected each other, and in eight weeks and countless nights, he'd become family, even if he didn't see it that way.

When the doors opened onto the eighteenth floor, Hannah tarried in the elevator. Then she pressed her eyes shut and replayed Jackson's last fall. She let the vision of his broken body burn into her eyelids and forced them open with a renewed determination. He was going to hate her, sure, but better that he hate her and remain whole than love her with the permanent injury she could've prevented. She'd rather he hate her than she hate herself.

"Hannah Bean?"

"Yep." Damn it. She was even starting to sound like him. Maybe that was okay, especially if it was all she was going to have left.

"He's waiting." The corporate receptionist gestured her in.

The door to Mr. Jacobs's office was heavy but Hannah pushed it aside, grateful for a resistance she could fight through easily. The Cardic exec stood and offered her a hand, which she accepted. "Miss Bean."

"I'd like to thank you for seeing me on such short

notice." She shifted from foot to foot and pressed her palms into the flesh of her thighs.

"You made it seem rather important." Mr. Jacobs raised an eyebrow and smiled. It was a presumptuous smile; the kind that left room and invited explanation.

It was now or never.

"I'm here regarding a contract. The contract with Brad Hill?"

"Brad Hill," Jacobs repeated, mouth twisting into a smirk. "Quite a handful that one, but favored to win the PRCA championships. Looks like we've bet on the right horse."

"He's in no shape to ride." The words tumbled from her mouth; she could no more stop them than she could stop breathing.

The smirk on his face disappeared as quickly as it had formed. She continued, for fear of losing her momentum. "That last fall, it left him with cracked vertebrae. He nearly broke his back—"

"But he didn't," Jacobs interjected.

"True. But if he takes another fall, anything, injuries would be permanent."

They were interrupted by the receptionist, who had poked her head in the door. "Your eleven o'clock is here," she said to Mr. Jacobs.

"I'll need a minute," Jacobs answered, shuffling the papers on his desk and eyeing Hannah. "We'll be done shortly."

The pending dismissal irked her. She took another step toward his desk and put a hand on her hip before cocking it forward, assuming utter confidence. "He can't ride."

"That's for the doctor to decide," Jacobs said.

"I am a doctor." Not for the first time, Hannah felt the swell of pride and added her second hand to her other hip, doubling down on her position.

"I thought you were the masseuse, the massage therapist?"

"A woman can be more than one thing. I took a short-term contract to allow myself some more insight into the tax this sport takes on a cowboy, and it is within my Hippocratic oath to speak out about this injury."

Jacobs looked at her with newfound respect. "What do you propose I do, Doctor?" he asked, careful to speak without a hint of sarcasm.

Hannah flushed, the heat spreading to her cheeks. "I didn't come here to tell you how to do your job…" she started.

"Didn't you?" Jacobs asked.

"If he rides, with your support, your company will be liable for any injury given that his medical realities have been disclosed by an attending physician. I'll leave you to your work and have my office follow up with the written notice of Mr. Hartmann's condition."

"You mean Mr. Hill. Mr. Hill's condition."

"Yes, right. Mr. Hill."

Jacobs studied her, putting down his pen and focusing all of his attention on her for the first time since she'd entered his office. "You said 'Mr. Hartmann.' That would be Jackson Hartmann, the younger of the brothers, the brother no one's seen on the public stage for ten years."

"I didn't say his name was Jackson," she muttered. "Listen, I have another appointment. I have to go."

"Mr. Jackson Hartmann. Riding under the alias of

Brad Hill." Jacobs picked up his pen again, tapping it against the pad.

As a doctor, Hannah knew it was impossible for blood to freeze. The human body worked in a perfect symphony of chemistry to keep the blood temperature at precisely the right heat to keep all things running in a miracle of science. But at that moment? At that moment, she felt her blood turn to ice. There was no way out. She'd slipped, and she'd slipped badly.

"Yes, of course. Mr. Hartmann, sure. I refer to him as Brad Hill to keep the rest of the team from knowing."

"I'll be in touch then, Dr. Bean. I'm sure we can find a way to restructure our cooperation to the benefit of all parties involved."

"Thanks." How she managed to utter even that one word while her mouth was so dry was beyond her. She nodded and left his office in the hope that her brisk pace would thaw her frozen limbs. She knew how important this race was to Jackson, but her medical opinion superseded his ego. There was no motivation worth the risk he was planning to take. She couldn't live with herself if he lost his ability to walk, let alone ride. She couldn't live with it. She'd rather lose him than watch him lose himself.

Still, as her heels clicked on the polished floor, the same thought echoed in her mind. *What had she done?*

There was something eerie about waiting for the guillotine to drop. She'd known it was a matter of time before he found her, and she'd practiced what to say, although the mirror offered little discourse in return.

The trailer had never felt smaller, but she forced a smile even as she heard the door jostle against weak hinges.

"They called. You had no right, no right at all, to do that." Rodney threw open the door to the trailer without invitation, his face red with anger.

Hannah swallowed. It was hardly how she'd imagined coming clean, but she was going to do it. If the rest of this conversation went as she anticipated, it would likely be her only chance.

"You've put everything at risk. Cardic has pulled out, but you know that. It's exactly what you wanted."

"What I wanted?" She reached for the glass of water on the counter and took a sip, any action to calm her nerves. It was easier to repeat his words than to string together her own.

"You overstepped. But this isn't over. He can still ride. If we bet the advance, we can make it all back. Earn the contract out even if it's gambling. Besides, it isn't gambling if you know you're gonna win." Rodney paced the trailer, shaking his head.

Hannah wondered who he was trying to convince.

"It's the ride of his career. You stole it from him."

Hannah took another sip of water. "Viper stole it from him," she corrected, keeping her voice calm.

"The hell he did." Rodney picked up her glass of water, made eye contact, then let it drop to the floor. "You're a doctor, and you disclosed private patient information. Pretty sure that goes against some sort of oath."

"I'm not just a doctor," she said as she rose to her feet. Rodney was mad. This wasn't going to go well. Her stomach twisted. But she didn't hold back. "I'm your daughter."

Rodney met her disclosure with a choked gasp. "I don't have a daughter."

"That's the thing. You do." She felt as if she stood outside herself. As if she were witnessing someone else admit a secret, the numbness of letting go setting her free.

"I don't have a daughter," he repeated. "And you? You don't have a job."

The words were a punch to her gut, but she was ready, muscles braced. She'd expected this, known it from the moment she'd stepped foot into Mr. Jacobs's office.

"You do have a daughter. It's why I came. To know you. And for you to know me. I want you in my life."

He looked at her and shook his head. "You ruined everything. Family is about priorities. Loyalty. You? You're a snitch."

Sometimes the closest family was the one you made for yourself, and she loved Jackson. Loved him enough to lose him. Maybe that was enough. Maybe eight weeks was enough to change her life.

As she followed Rodney out the door, deeply aware of his threats and promises to put her on a bus to Bozeman, she smiled. Yes, it was better to have loved and lost than never to have loved at all. If she had to do it all again, she would.

Even the memory of Jackson Hartmann would be enough to make it all worth it. To belong even for a few weeks was better than to never have belonged at all.

"I'm getting old." Jackson grabbed the base of his back. It hurt, but nothing he couldn't handle. Will was drinking Scotch, but Jackson refused to drink any hard alcohol before noon. It seemed a small step of propriety, but an important one. Indeed, if ever there'd been a time to drink, it was now, as he nursed the ache in his chest he stubbornly refused to address.

"You said it, old man," Willie answered, grinning.

He wasn't going to think about her. Not anymore. That was done. All he had left to think about was Mayhem and his upcoming ride, six days from now.

He heard Rodney before he saw him.

"That little interfering bitch." He was cursing, spitting his insults across the diner. "Two-timing traitorous piece of—"

"Hey, man, this is a family place," Jackson said, cutting him off. Jackson's eyes were fixed on a skinny ten-year-old boy attracted by the loud cursing of the crusty cowpoke. A slim woman, presumably the boy's mother, glared at Rodney and then, by association, Jackson. He flashed a smile of apology, which did little to soften the glare.

Rodney slid into the booth and slapped his phone down on the table. "Boy, you're not gonna believe who just called me."

"I'm guessing we're not gonna have to wait long to find out?" Jackson smiled, amused by Rodney's aggressive unhappiness.

"She did this. She's responsible."

If Jackson knew anything, it was that Rodney likely deserved whatever punishment this anonymous "she" had dished out.

"It's over," Rodney lamented, his anger turning to sorrow. The change turned Jackson's appetite. He pushed his plate of eggs toward Willie, who tucked into the rest of Jackson's breakfast with enthusiasm.

"I'm sure it's not as bad as all that." Jackson was surprised he was comforting Rodney after all of their recent issues.

"It's worse." Rodney's head sank into his hands. Then, with a snap decision, his head jerked up and he barked an order to a nearby waitress. "I'll have a beer."

"I'm feeling fine. Better than I thought I'd feel. Only one more ride, and don't worry your pretty little head." Sure, the words felt hollow, but it didn't make them less true. It would be fun to ride. No expiration girlfriend was in a position to challenge a goal he'd carried with him for well over a decade. What was eight weeks in the face of seventeen years?

"It's over, Brad."

The words washed over him like a tide. "Over?" The din of the diner quieted and all Jackson could hear was his own pulse. Throbbing in his ears and his wrists. *Over?*

"The call this morning. Been trying to work a way around it ever since."

"'Work around it'?" Jacks repeated as though the echo would somehow bring some clarity.

"Can't do it. It's done. Cardic pulled this morning. Pulled out. They aren't backing you for the PRCA, so there's no point."

There it was. With one sentence, his independence, his ability to make a name for himself that wasn't linked to the past his father had saddled them with, all came crashing down.

"Why?" Surprisingly, it was Willie who managed

to voice the question that echoed in Jackson's mind. Then he found his own voice and repeated the question himself.

"Yeah, why?"

"Her."

He didn't need to say more. One word and the truth crashed around him. The deception. The betrayal. For a brief moment, he wished the "her" in question was a different one than the woman he cared about so deeply.

"Not sure I'm following," Wille interrupted again.

"The massage therapist. She is also a doctor, as you know." The waitress arrived with his beer, and Rodney tilted the drink up, swallowing it in loud gulps.

"She's a resident," Jackson corrected. It felt necessary to cling to some semblance of truth through all the lies.

Willie let out a low whistle and tipped his hat back off his brow. "That's a lot." Then, with an uncharacteristic ability to read the room, he focused his attention back to the remains of Jackson's breakfast.

"Whatever you want to call her, she's a traitor. Now that she's disclosed your injuries to Cardic, they dropped you. Their contract team is looking into the sponsorship and they'll get back to us with the required revisions. But you're not riding on their banner. Something about legal liability. You know, like, if you get injured, and they gotta look after you for the rest of your life if you end up sucking your dinner down from a straw." Rodney rolled his eyes.

"Quite the picture you're painting there, Rod," Jackson managed to speak over his twisting stomach. He was mad. Mad and, perhaps, if he was ready to face the sliver of honesty he'd been denying, a little relieved.

"Goes with the job, the odd injury or two." Rodney launched into his sales pitch, the same one he'd regurgitated time and time again.

"To be fair, it's not really a mild injury. It's a spinal fracture, but I can still ride. With or without the Cardic sponsorship, I can ride." Jacks frowned. Then, taking in the frozen expression on Willie's face as he held his fork suspended midair in shock, he brushed away the concern. He wasn't the kind of cowboy that shied away from danger. Hell, danger was precisely the currency he traded in. Danger was his brand.

Across the table, Rodney reached for his phone. He started typing, the keys clicking furiously.

"Who are you texting?" Willie asked, relieving Jackson of having to ask himself.

"Just telling Hannah. I want her to know she failed. Now she'll lose her license for nothing, that little liar."

Jackson bristled. "That's enough, Rodney," he threatened. The swoosh from Rod's phone ignited an anger in Jackson he struggled to control. "I *can* still ride. I didn't say I was going to." He shifted gears. "Where is she?"

At his question, Rodney's lips curled in a smirk. He looked down at his watch, bleary-eyed, and the smile deepened. "Right now? I imagine she's getting close to Butte. I put her on the bus this morning. Right after I fired her."

The slam of cutlery on the adjacent tabletop was aggressive, and the neighboring mother and child stood, muttering under their breaths. Then they left.

"I best be going too." Jackson stood, peeled two twenties from his money clip, throwing the bills into the center of the table. "That oughta cover breakfast," he managed to say. He didn't believe it. Didn't believe for a minute she was gone just like that on the bus. It couldn't be true. If Hannah had been willing to put her license on the line, maybe he needed to rethink things.

Willie interrupted him before he could walk away from the table. He let out a whistle after glancing at the newspaper beside his plate. "You're famous," he told Jackson.

Jackson scanned the front page of the *Gazette* and his heart fell to his stomach.

"Brad Hill is favored to win, but unnamed sources behind his Cardic sponsorship reveal the rodeo champ is none other than the lost Hartmann heir, Jackson Hartmann," he read aloud.

Willie and Rodney stared, open-mouthed, across the table, then Rodney snatched the paper away.

"Well, now you have to ride," he said. "He can leverage this press into very favorable odds."

Jackson stared at the back of the paper, body flooded with emotion. Now, if he competed, risked everything for eight seconds, it would be to win as a Hartmann. That meant he couldn't win at all.

The room that met him was empty. The bed had been made, not by the maid service, he could tell as much by the sloppy corners, but by her. Who else would make the bed in a hotel room? His body betrayed him by smiling. He shouldn't be amused by her. Shouldn't think even for a minute that she was cute. She was like those mushrooms, the kind that look so enticing with their fairy-tale red-and-white heads poking out from canopies of thick moss. Those mushrooms? The cute ones? They kill you. End you.

He saw the note next. He hadn't been looking for it, but it was tough not to see it laid out on his side of the bed so purposefully as to not be ignored.

Jackson,
I don't expect you to understand. Hell, I'm not even sure I understand. I know you probably hate me right now. How could you not? But it has to be this way. I couldn't live with the stakes you were willing to gamble.

I've been dreading our expiration. I've been afraid of it. Afraid of how I would continue the charade, because we were a charade, or at least, it was a charade for me. Pretending I can set any sort of expiration to the way I feel about you.

I only hope you can understand how important these eight weeks were to me. The only thing that comes close were the few days I had left, so you can imagine how tough it was to pay that price. I knew confronting you about your injuries, forcing your hand with Cardic, would end us. But I would do it again to keep you safe.

I would do it all again.
Yours,
Hannah

He crunched the letter into a ball and threw it across the room, surprised by his own ferocity. He ran a hand through his hair then shook his head. Then he walked around the bed, bent, picked up the paper and un-crimped it. Jackson. She'd addressed the letter to Jackson. So she still thought he could be him. That he *should* be him. That he should abandon Brad and be Jackson again, this time for real.

The sick feeling mounted, flooding his mouth with the acrid taste of bile.

He reached for his phone and cursed. There was only one person he could call. Only one person who could help. Problem was, it was the last person he wanted to speak to.

"Nick here," his brother answered a little too cheerily.

"We gotta talk," Jackson announced.

Thirteen

Fired & Expired

"You mean I'm to ride with the paramedic team?" Hannah asked. Roberta, the cheery head of HR at Bozeman General, was clearly out to lunch.

"Yes, our triage team is light for the next three weeks. If you could help to bridge that gap, it would be no issue to advance your start date."

To be fair, triage was still medicine, and she had done a placement in ER, so it wasn't out of the question. "Thanks a lot. I really appreciate your flexibility." Hannah offered her gratitude robotically, grateful the phone offered some distance between the administrator and herself. Any moment of self-doubt would not be seen.

"Not at all. This actually suits the hospital wonderfully since they're short-staffed. We're really looking forward to you joining us, Dr. Bean." The HR director disconnected the call with the promise of having all the paperwork in order for tomorrow morning at ten. So that was one thing sorted at least.

Hannah exhaled. Here she was, on the same Greyhound bus. On the same bus, and in the same place she'd been before taking the position as a staff masseuse. Two short months and the only thing different was her. Her effort to get to know her dad had grounded her in failure. He didn't want her; just wanted to see her fail. He hadn't even flinched when she'd told him the truth.

In their final showdown, in that final moment when her own dad was firing her for her honesty, she'd lost the courage to fight back.

"Rodney, I'm your daughter." She said the words now to no one in particular. They didn't sound scary. But earlier? They had been terrifying.

There was something about Rodney himself that made it all the more disappointing. Truth was, she didn't care, or at least she didn't want to care anymore. He wasn't the father figure she'd hoped to find, but she reminded herself she'd found something better. Well, found it then lost it. Found him and lost him.

Jackson.

She bit her lip and chewed on the thought.

The jolting bus was far less luxurious than Jackson's top-of-the-line Cardic. Worse still, there wasn't a broody cowboy driving with a maddening dimple peeking out to flirt with her every time he cracked a smile.

Now, as the bus drove toward Bozeman, it was raining. She closed her eyes for a moment, reliving another night in the rain: the first time he'd kissed her. That was all she had now. Memories.

Her phone was a welcome interruption to the self-pity she clung to.

"Emily. Emily. Emily," she muttered after a cursory glance at the caller ID.

"Are you okay, Hannah?"

Hannah watched as the rain slid down her window. "Am I okay?" she repeated. She couldn't answer even if she wanted to.

She didn't know.

"I really thought this was going to go differently. With him." Emily sighed. Her voice was quiet and Hannah pressed her eyes shut to focus on the reassurance of her best friend.

"Me too." Hannah gritted her teeth in a determination not to cry. She wasn't about to cry on a Greyhound bus.

"You can still tell him. There's no expiration on honesty," Emily asserted, shining in yet another moment of logic.

"He's gonna ride. Against my medical advice. And worse than that, Em, he's deliberately choosing the risk. Deliberately choosing the alias. Over me." She saw Rodney's triumphant text, burned in her brain. She'd seen the newspaper article. Read it a thousand times. Damn it.

"What about Rodney?"

"Rodney doesn't matter. This is about Jackson. With Jackson, I felt whole. I felt seen." She paused then dug deep for bravery. "I felt loved."

It was the last admission that broke the dam and let loose a flood of tears that streamed silently down her face. Across the aisle, an elderly woman pursed her lips in disapproval. The woman's hair was pulled back in a severe bun, powder gray, and, following the stony stare, she turned her attention back to a book.

"That's why you did it. That's why you compromised your damn medical license?"

"Doesn't change anything. I would do it again," Hannah admitted dully.

"That's the worst part. Even now, when I come at you with facts, you don't even deny it." Emily was exasperated.

"Some people consider it rude to talk on the phone in public," the old woman interrupted.

Hannah glared at her, issuing an ice-cold stare of her own. "Some people should mind their own business," she answered icily.

"If you think telling me to mind my own business is gonna help you, even for a second, you've got another think coming. I've half a mind to get on a plane to Bozeman right now." Emily was livid.

"I'm not talking to you, Em. You need to stay in Boston," she explained. Then she stifled a sob. "It's done. There is no going back. If you think I would stand aside while Jackson got on the back of another bucking bull while there's still a breath left in my body, you, him and anyone else in my way would have a rude awakening. He might not value his life enough to fight for it, but I sure as hell do." She swallowed, feeling strength return with the force of her conviction.

"What about your dad? Maybe if you talk to Rodney, you can avoid a complaint. I can't imagine Jackson would press charges—"

But it wasn't her license that had Hannah so fraught

with emotion. "What do you think I should do? What can I do now? This thing I had with Jackson, it was bigger than me. Maybe not for him." She paused then added, "But it was for me." She whispered into the phone, acutely aware of her disgruntled neighbor.

"I know. I know you had something special, but you can't go down with this ship, Hannah. Look, you need to get in touch with your dad. With no complaint, there is no consequence, and you've worked far too hard to lose your license. While there is still a breath left in my body, I am not gonna let that happen, even if I have to confront HotRod myself."

The confidence with which her friend proposed her plan evoked a confidence of her own. "Okay," Hannah said. She could do this. "I'll think about it."

Emily disconnected before Hannah could protest, but it was just as well. There was something to be said for strength in numbers, and at present, Hannah had never felt more alone.

Nick and Jacks rode in silence, the horses guided by a squeeze of thigh. Jackson rode Outlaw, whose coat shone in the moonlight.

"Nice horse you've got there," Nick offered.

"Yep," Jackson agreed. Outlaw was a fine horse.

"I don't know what brought you here early, Jackson, but I must say I'm glad."

Jackson clicked his tongue and Outlaw sprang into a trot, leaving Nick behind. He could hear the clip of hooves behind and took comfort in the fact that Nick was following suit. He knew exactly where to go.

Twenty minutes later, they were there.

"It looks the same," Jackson stated, nodding at the headstone.

"Yep." It was Nick's turn to issue monosyllabic responses.

The family plot was at the top of a rolling hill, at the crest of which was planted a lone tree, an elm, with a trunk larger than a barrel. A wrought-iron fence rusted around the perimeter of the family plot, the intricate scrolls and twists over a century old. Family headstones dated back well over a century, from a time before Montana was even a state. The script had worn off the older monuments, but not off the freshest four. His mother and father. His big brother Austin and his wife, Katherine, buried only a year prior.

Jackson sat in front of Elma's grave. He didn't remember his mom—his first mom. Josephine had raised him. Had been his mother for all intents and purposes. But still, in the quiet of the night, Jackson allowed himself to wonder if his birth mom's death hadn't severed a part of his father. How many of the men in the Hartmann family had cleaved apart the night Elma died?

Nick stood over their father's grave. It was well maintained.

"Cody keeps the place clean. He trims the plants, that sort of thing." Nick tipped his eyes to the plot.

"Sure." Jackson swallowed. It was hard to accept that it was Cody, the head wrangler, doing the sons' duty, but from the pained look in Nick's eyes, it was easy to assume this wasn't any simpler for him.

"Are you still mad?" Nick asked quietly. "At them?"

Jackson studied Bart's grave then closed his eyes.

He could hear her as clearly as if she were in front of him, telling him off with her stern accent.

Do you think an honorable man would turn his back on the kind of legacy that could change his family forever? The kind of legacy that could change him?

"I don't want to be," Jackson confessed. "I really don't want to be mad anymore." He'd rather fight for a new legacy, or whatever the heck Hannah had spoken about.

"You don't have to be." Nick threw a heavy arm around his brother. "Let's make a new home."

"'A new home'?" Jacks repeated the thought aloud, as though voicing it himself offered a new perspective. What did that even mean? Roots? A family? All the things he'd never allowed himself to want? "I won't fit in here, Nick. I'm not the family kind of guy," he finished a little lamely.

Nick brushed some moss off Elma's grave. "I don't come here enough. Don't come here ever really. Except when Rose insists. Or with Alix. Actually, maybe I do come here enough." He let out a dry laugh in an attempt to add some levity to the confession.

"But what I've learned, with Rose and Alix, is that we can make our own family. We can make our own rules, our own roots. And I am one thousand percent sure about one thing, Jackson, and that is you *do* belong here. With me. Hartmann brothers on the land we tamed."

Jackson didn't answer. His voice was thick with emotion and he didn't trust it. He just smiled at his big brother and nodded. Hartmann brothers. It had a nice ring to it.

"What do you say, maybe we get you into the west wing? You can have it to yourself. Or you can share it with someone?" Nick raised an eyebrow in inquiry.

Jackson offered a quick jab into his brother's ribs and managed a smile. "Why don't I start moving in just on my own? Baby steps."

"Speaking of babies…" Nick's voice trailed off as he headed toward his horse, swinging a leg over the stallion and mounting with a swift ease.

"I beg your pardon?" Jackson flushed. Surely, Boston wasn't pregnant? Nick didn't know something he didn't know, did he?

"Rose is pregnant," Nick admitted. "You're going to be an uncle again, so I'm glad to hear you'll stick around for this one. This kid is going to need someone to show him the ropes and teach him the land."

Jackson pasted a smile on his face then offered the expected congratulations, all the while wondering why he'd jumped right to thoughts of Hannah and a baby of their own.

She had been right. About his family. About his place. Maybe she was even right about him being enough. If he could be enough for her, it would be enough for him. It was hard to believe he was standing on Hartmann land, a stone's throw from his father's grave, wanting to start fresh.

And yet, under the moonlight, it dawned on him.

He did.

Fourteen

Mamma Mia

"Nice to have you back," Amelia admitted, kicking at the overgrown grass threatening the neat grooming of their otherwise perfectly manicured lawn.

"Yep," Jackson agreed. The trek from the house to the barn was just shy of a quarter of a mile, and they walked shoulder to shoulder on the path.

Amelia was put together. If you weren't looking for it, you wouldn't notice. The tightening of the muscle at her lip. The clenched jaw. The hair pulled back a little too severely. She didn't smile, hadn't smiled, since he'd arrived.

"You could have told me." She kicked at the path again.

"I couldn't have. Remember, I know you."

She bristled beside him. "Know you? Ha, I thought I did." Another wave of gravel sprayed onto the lawn, her leather riding boot effective at broadcasting her displeasure.

"Mia, come on, don't be like that. I had to get out of there. Dad wanted me to be a pretty face. A celebrity politician."

"Ah, I get it. You think riding rodeo as a celebrity is somehow better."

Ouch, she had him there.

"I earned that celebrity." He took a turn at kicking gravel. "It was never supposed to be like that."

"It never is," Amelia agreed. Then she stopped. "We need you here, Jacks. I get it. I mean it was bad for you. But it was worse without you."

Her admission caught him off guard with its depth.

"Well, I'm back now." He swallowed gruffly. *And it felt good.*

"Are you? Are you really? Nick told me about the girl."

"The girl?" She meant Hannah. Couldn't mean anyone else. "Hannah. That's complicated."

It was hard to be with someone who pushed you to be the best version of yourself, but for her it might be worth it.

"You don't need to explain it to me, I get it." She brushed him away.

"Get it?" He paused. "Get what?" The sun was out and shone hot against them. He felt his phone vibrate in his pocket, more persistent than a pesky mosquito. He pressed his eyes shut and hoped it was her.

"I get that it's easier being alone. Cleaner. And I totally agree."

It wasn't the permissive support he'd been expecting. If anything, her blasé attitude served only to frustrate him. "Agree? Agree that I made the right choice, fighting with the only woman I've ever met who had the courage to stand up to me? To actually change my mind?" He surprised himself with his vehemence.

"Maybe other women could have changed your mind if you'd let them try," Amelia shot back.

"I get it. I get it. I left and I'm bad and mean and all the rest of it. I was seventeen. It was self-preservation." He raised his hands in defense.

"Wouldn't you like that?" She turned and squared her shoulders to his. "Wouldn't that be easy, just sweep it all under the rug, the way you left me, now coming back ten years later, pretending you're different than he is?"

Damn. Amelia was right. He had turned out just like dear old dad. Not to his own kids, but to his kid sister. And the realization was devastating.

"Mia, I'm sorry." He pulled her into his arms, crushed her against his chest. "I was so wrapped up. So stupid and hurting, and the last thing I wanted was not to be there for you. You're right. Hannah's right."

The last part of his confession was to himself. But that didn't make it less true.

Amelia's body was rigid in his embrace. He pulled her tighter. "I'm sorry, sis. Really. I'm here now."

"Until when?" Her voice was muffled as she spoke into his chest.

"Until forever," Jackson assured. Suddenly he felt lighter, and not just because his little sister was smiling for the first time since he'd been home. Was it really possible that all he'd been looking for his entire life had been here all along? That the only bucking bulls he'd needed to conquer were his own demons? Hannah had drawn back the curtain and shown him something more important than pride.

Love.

"Your phone is blowing up," Amelia noted, her tone completely devoid of sarcasm or any emotion. Nick had been right about one thing: the clearheaded Amelia was a shell of herself. But he was back, and the new order of the day was to fix all things broken by the Hartmann clan. His own mishaps included.

Jackson reached into his pocket and frowned as he registered the twelve missed calls from Rodney. He'd hoped they were from Hannah. Prayed they were.

"You gonna answer or what?" she asked.

"I'll call him back." He stopped before he could drop the phone into his pocket. "Actually, maybe I'll give him a quick call now." He dialed Rodney, wondering what issue could have necessitated twelve calls. They arrived at the barn, and Mia pulled open the door.

"Whatever, I'm going riding," Amelia called over her shoulder as she turned her back and made her way to the stall at the back where her silver mare shook a silky mane in her direction. Before Jackson could correct her, she had one leg in the stirrup.

"I did it," Rodney said right before he launched into a self-satisfied laugh without waiting for standard niceties.

"Did what?" Jackson countered, staring after the barn doors his sister had exited moments earlier.

"I filed a complaint on your behalf, with the licensing board." Rodney cursed. "I still can't believe we got so close."

It was annoying, the way Rodney flung around a pejorative "we" as though Jackson's rodeo success was in some way due to him. Apart from negotiating the contract, the magic was all his. All Brad's. Rather, Jackson's.

"She didn't mean anything by it," he said. The defense was easier to make now that there was space between them. Between Brad and Jackson. Now that he knew which side he was meant to live on.

"Didn't mean anything by it? She ended you." Rodney was outraged. "The good news, at least, is that with the media interest in the 'long-lost Hartmann,' we've got an even bigger purse on the line. Guess that's not really gonna motivate you though."

Ha, good news for who? The advance was peanuts for a Hartmann; Rodney was right about that.

"Just so you know, it's different without you here. Your friends miss you. Most of them still can't believe they had ranch royalty living among them, a real 'man of the people' if you will."

"Yeah, I'm a real Cinderella Man."

He missed them too. Willie, Mikey. A whole bunch.

"Cinderella Man, that's cute. You sayin' there's no way I can change your mind?"

Rodney was referring to Jackson's refusal to ride. The fight had been explosive, resulting in Jackson's departure from the camp. Rodney had taken Jackson in as a young man, but there was no denying that at some point their relationship had gotten lost. And now? How could he stand by the man who was intent on relieving Hannah of her medical license?

"There might be one way to salvage things with Cardic Motors."

Jackson flirted with the idea. If he were very careful, he could maybe kill two birds with one stone.

"Do all the ER doctors make house calls with the paramedics?" Hannah asked, flustered as she was jostled in the back of the ambulance.

She was strapped in on the bench next to a hydraulic bed and a series of beeping machines. But at least the interior was a comfortable relief from the otherwise sticking August heat.

"When the house in question built the hospital, we go. Any call from Hartmann Ranch and it's white-glove service." Eric, the paramedic, was holding back a smile.

"Hartmann. We're going to Hartmann Homestead?" Hannah swallowed. It was a heck of a second day on the job.

"Amelia was thrown from her horse. She looks fine but the boss said to send us out. We've got a fundraising gala in a month and the Hartmanns have six tables reserved already. So out we go." Eric shrugged as though a twenty-minute ambulance ride was nothing out of the ordinary. It certainly felt another lifetime away from Boston.

"Any vitals from the scene?" She searched valiantly for a mask, eager to hide behind protocol.

"Steady. This is routine, a little blood loss, broken bone, but they've got pressure on the wound."

"Right. Okay." Hannah pressed her back against the

wall of the ambulance, swearing the back of her shirt was starting to stick to the cold metal. Then again, maybe the cold would calm her nerves. Why hadn't she worn makeup today? Or gone for a blowout?

"I told you dressing like a doctor was a bad idea," Emily chastened.

She'd jumped into the ambulance moments before it departed. "I just finished a placement in trauma. I'd better come," she'd told the driver.

No one in the ambulance had had the time or presence of mind to question why a visiting doctor had wanted to come along, but Hannah reached for the hand of her best friend and squeezed it. "I'm glad you're here," she admitted without making eye contact.

Emily didn't say anything, just fished a lipstick out from the pocket of her scrubs. "Adore Me," she whispered. "It's my favorite shade. It'll be gorgeous with your hair."

Eric rolled his eyes from across the ambulance and Emily shot him a silencing gaze.

Hannah didn't say anything; just accepted the lipstick and put on her armor. His family would be there. And she had no idea what to say or how to act. Still, as she stared out the window at the rear of the ambulance, watching as they left the city behind them, she couldn't help but fight back a smile.

They arrived on the scene without enough time for Hannah to take in the opulence of the estate. She was moving quickly, the surroundings passing in flashes that barely registered.

Jackson opened the doors to the ambulance, reaching for the bed and helping Eric pull it from the vehicle.

"She's over there," he barked at the entourage.

"Over there" was north of the barn. A large structure painted white, with pewter trim, that towered over the fantasies and images sketched by her imagination. The barn was nestled at the edge of a fenced yard, where horses stomped on raked soil. It was a working ranch, with cowboys riding and animal noises assaulting her senses. But she didn't see any of it. She was frozen by him.

"Mr. Hartmann," Emily interrupted. "Dr. Barrett here. What can you tell me about your sister's injury?" If the Boston accent caught Jackson off guard, he didn't show it.

Jackson broke the stare she felt in her bones, and tipped his head toward Emily. "Yes, of course. Amelia is a practiced horsewoman, but her mount threw her within minutes of her leaving the barn. Still, pretty sure her break will need setting." He gestured toward Amelia Hartmann, who was sitting with her back against an elm trunk, stiff upper lip holding back tears.

"Is that your medical opinion?" Emily pressed a little coldly.

"No, you're right. I just believed, since the bone had punctured the skin, it was safe to assume there had been a break." Jackson matched Emily's tone chill for chill. Then his eyes met Hannah's. His eyes, honey-colored and clear, saw through her, and she wondered for a moment if her heart was visible through her scrubs.

Hannah allowed herself one minute of staring back. One minute of sinking into the warm eyes that held her through some of the most intense feelings of her life. Of love. Belonging. Acceptance. But when she'd tried to help him, tried to be there for him the way family would? Should? When she'd tried to really help him make good decisions? He'd left her. Cast her aside, and she wasn't stupid enough to put herself in that position again. She couldn't, stares and longing be damned.

"Hi, Amelia. I'm Hannah and I'm here to help you."

"Is Silver okay?" Amelia asked without acknowledging the offer of help. Amelia held her hand pressed tight into her chest.

"The horse is fine," Jackson assured her. He crouched next to Amelia, his long legs folding awkwardly as he knelt in a deep squat.

Hannah smiled, appreciating the depth of patience Jackson showed his sister. He reached toward Mia's shoulder, offering a fleeting squeeze.

"Well, go and be with her. She's probably scared." Amelia dismissed her big brother with a facility that made Hannah jealous. If only she, too, could dismiss him with such ease.

"Yes, go," she echoed. "This will be easier without you in the way."

Just like that, Hannah dismissed him too.

Check on the horse? Of all the infernal suggestions... Jackson looked back over his shoulder, watching two of the most important women in his life confer. Amelia's face had relaxed and, for the first time in a little over a week, Jackson saw his sister smile. Of course she was smiling, she was looking at Hannah.

"Better get these guys back to work." Jackson looked

around the barn, wondering why the cowboys were hanging around.

"I think everyone just wants to make sure Miss Mia is okay," Cody said.

"I reckon there're likely much more important things for you cowpokes to be doing," Emily chided. As the ranch hands scattered, Jackson spun to meet the engaged smile of the doctor who had initially seen to his sister.

"Jackson. Jackson Hartmann," he said as he extended a hand to the tall woman in the lab coat.

"I'm just surprised you didn't introduce yourself as Brad."

"Likely as surprised as I am to hear another Boston accent in this neck of the woods. The world feels quite small to allow for these coincidences, don't you think?"

Emily laughed and, just like that, the tough girl façade cracked apart. "I'm Hannah's best friend. And yes, before you ask, I know all about you. All about you and her loser dad…" She was still grinning and babbling on and on in a prattling run-on of excited chatter, but Jackson didn't hear any of it.

"Loser dad?" He thrust his hands in his pockets but didn't shy away from her gaze. Emily froze, but Jackson wasn't going to let the pretty doctor worm her way out of this one. She'd let too much slip and he knew it.

"I think they need me." Emily tilted her head toward Hannah and Amelia, both of whom were chatting while Hannah took his sister's pulse.

"You're not going anywhere," he told her, "not until you tell me what you meant by 'loser dad.'"

"Are you seriously pretending that you don't know?

That you haven't the faintest idea why Hannah would stick around eight weeks with that slob instead of taking a premium position at a top-notch hospital where people actually respect her medical opinion?"

He grimaced. Her indignation hit a little close to home. "Hey, I respect her medical opinion."

"Except that you didn't. Except that you thought it would be better to put dear old Hannah in a position where she would compromise her medical license all for the sake of your spine. You know, I thought I could do this. I thought I could come here and pretend. But I'm over it. Over this façade—"

"Em," called a warmer voice.

Hannah.

"Right, er, I'll go and check on the team." Emily, whom Jackson gathered was not often at a loss for words, spun and left.

"You gonna tell me?" He asked the question without turning to look at her, wondering for a moment if it would be easier for them to talk without the electricity that sparked every time they locked eyes.

"Tell you what? That I'm the product of a one-night stand? And that Rodney—good old HotRod—is my dear old dad?" Her voice choked, and Jackson willed himself not to turn and pull her into a crushing hug.

"I threw it away. Disappointed him. Ended any chance we might have had a relationship. All for you." Hannah took a few steps forward, and soon she was looking straight at Jackson. "And you? You watched me burn it all down."

Jackson, in an effort to make sense of everything, grabbed her arm.

"Let go of me." Hannah shook him off, the act requiring little effort as he did not persist.

"I had no idea about HotRod. I didn't really know about any of it."

"Well, now you know. Question is, cowboy, what are you going to do about it?" And with that haunting question, a tear broke free.

Jackson stared. It made sense. Her horrifying family history, the importance she placed on family. She was self-made, and risking everything she'd earned, everything she'd wanted, to stop him from being reckless. To get him to see that he was enough, at least for her. And if he could be enough for her...

"I don't know what to say," he admitted. All he wanted to do was to tell her she was everything, but with the threat of a suspended medical license, and his stubbornness to blame, he couldn't say the three words his mind screamed.

At his silence, Hannah left the barn.

"Hannah," he called after her.

"No, Jackson. You win. You broke me." She said it as she walked to the ambulance, past the stretcher holding Amelia.

The ride to Bozeman was quiet, with only a few steady beeps from the machine nearby. Emily and Hannah sat strapped into the back of the ambulance in stilted silence, while Amelia lay on the stretcher.

"Hannah." Amelia broke the silence.

"Yes?" Hannah managed to answer, despite her shock.

"With all due respect, I think you're wrong about my brother. I think you're actually the one who broke him."

Hannah sucked in a breath, wondering for a moment if she should be coy and pretend not to know what Amelia was referring to. She couldn't. "Broke him? I didn't break anything."

"But you did. Jackson used to be wild. Now he is simpering after an ER doctor, of all things." Amelia rolled her eyes. "You're not much better," she said through a smile. "I saw you simper earlier too."

So, she had heard. Hannah had thought as much. But she didn't feel embarrassed at having been overheard. She just felt empty. Was this what it was going to be? Living without him? An emptiness that threatened to last forever?

Hannah couldn't help but wonder for a moment if it were possible. If his own sister had noticed a change in him, maybe it wasn't too late. She could've sworn she'd seen a flash in his eyes when they'd met hers. A flash that had left her feeling uncertain if there was a future between them. Heck, as far she was concerned, they could live under a tent as long as they were together. Now it was time to fight.

She stared at Hartmann Homestead through the back windows of the ambulance, watching as the ranch got smaller and smaller. She'd shocked him with the news of Rodney. And silence was a normal reaction, a medically explainable reaction, to shock. She might've lost her father, but what if she'd found her family?

Fifteen

Home

"I still don't see why we're doing this, but it's your money," Rodney mumbled as he stirred the sugar into his cafeteria coffee.

"That's right. It's my money." Jackson swallowed. It had been easier to get Rodney to agree to meet than he'd anticipated. He'd offered the one thing that had always motivated Rodney. Cash.

"Well, I'm here. What was so important we needed to talk about it face-to-face? And in a hospital nonetheless? Do you have news?" Rodney offered an exaggerated once-over toward Jackson's back then raised his brows.

Jackson studied the man seated opposite him. Rodney was not a bad man, and he was looking tired. His face was heavily lined from years in the sun and perhaps too many nights of hard living. But underneath it all was still the gruff softy that had taken him in over a decade ago. He had a good side, Jackson reminded himself for the millionth time. The trick was luring it out.

Jackson leaned forward on the table, resting his weight on his forearms, and locked eyes with his former manager. Best get to it.

"You filed a complaint against Hannah with the medical board. But you were not directly implicated in that complaint. This fight is mine. The disclosure is also my business. I need you to drop everything, effective immediately."

Jackson reached for his coffee and swallowed the bitter liquid. It still felt surreal, finally saying it aloud. It wasn't lost on him that Hannah had risked her medical license to defend his ability to walk. The realization had never been clearer than now, as Jackson sat in front of the man who was ready to levy the punishment for her courage. Could there be a truer act of love than to sacrifice your own gift to protect another's? It dawned on him then, under the too-bright lights of the cafeteria. Hannah Bean really must love him. The feeling filled his chest with an unexpected tightness.

"Pffft. You'd have me give up? Let her get away with it? After she robbed you of our dream?" Rodney asked.

"It's not my dream anymore. I get that you worked hard, helped to get me here." Jackson shrugged, unsure of how to frame their new relationship. "I'm going to make sure you are appropriately compensated for that."

"That'll take more than the two hundred fifty you promised me to get to this coffee date." Rodney dragged a hand through his patchy hair then across his beard. "Look, kid. Females, they can confuse you. I just want to make sure you're not giving up on your dream. I know how hard you worked. I know how gifted you are. I just don't want to see you lose everything. You earned this chance."

Just like that, Jackson felt seventeen again. This was the Rodney he knew. The Rodney who had a soft spot the size of Montana, if you only had the map to find it. He smiled. "That's why we're here. Because I don't want to lose everything."

Rodney exhaled a long, calm breath.

"I need you to make this right, Rodney. Make it right, and we can still work together. But our cooperation? It starts with Hannah. You make things right with her. And you do it now." He debated a moment about coming clean, about mentioning her lineage, but decided against it.

Jackson had kept his voice quiet as he'd delivered the message, hoping it wouldn't come across as an order. He studied Rodney, overwhelmed by the look on the older man's face. Relief. Life was hard on the road, maybe it was his own fault for not seeing it sooner. The PRCAs were more than a challenge for Jackson, they were the way out for Rodney. The purse that made a difference to the older man's retirement. Well, so be it. The man would always have a spot in the Hartmann bunkhouse, if Jackson had anything to say about it. He was sure of one thing. Family didn't leave family hanging, and whether he liked it or not, Rodney was Hannah's family.

"Right. We always were a great team, Brad. I mean..."

Rodney cleared his throat and added a shy "Jackson" to punctuate the sentiment.

Jackson nodded, but before he could answer, Rodney continued.

"You have something special, son. It makes sense. That you're a Hartmann, I mean. You never did quite fit in with us, and I can see why. You have a real gift, a fight I haven't seen much in my career. She's got it too. The woman's a spitfire. I get it. If I'm being honest, I guess I'm jealous. Jealous she had the courage to do what I didn't. Shouldn'ta come to her to make that call. I let you down, Jackson. I let you down, but she had your back. I'll drop the complaint, if it's what you want."

Jackson felt his jaw go slack. Of all the things he'd been thinking Rodney would say, admitting jealousy was the last thing he'd expected. He looked at his watch the same moment that her voice broke the silence.

"Jackson," she called.

Once again, Jackson heard her before he saw her. Her voice crossed the room like a breath of fresh air. His relief, even at hearing her voice, was amazing.

In moments, Hannah was at the table, a cloud crossing her face. She looked adorable in scrubs, the light blue matching her clear gaze.

"Hannah. I know it's not my place." Jackson gestured from Rodney to her.

The cloud on her brow turned her face from hopeful optimism to a wretched understanding. "I see. You invited me here to see *him*."

Perhaps his text message, inviting her to a quick lunch to discuss Amelia, had been a tad misleading.

However, he had wanted to be sure she'd come. Desperate times…

Hannah pulled on the lapels of her white lab coat, summoning courage from the uniform. "Actually, I'm glad you're here. We've got unfinished business."

Jackson slid across the booth, offering some space for her to sit, but she shook her head and glared at Rodney. "I'm a doctor. No one helped me get here, not really. I'm a doctor and I'm so proud of that." Her voice was strong and clear.

"You know the difference between God and a doctor? God knows he's not a doctor." Rodney guffawed and rolled his eyes, then moved his legs before Jackson could deliver a warning jab.

Hannah ignored him and continued. "He couldn't ride. You—" she said as she turned to Jackson. "You couldn't ride, and you wouldn't listen. And I? I didn't have a choice. And no, before you ask, I'm not sorry. I'd do it all again, just the same."

"You had a choice all right," Rodney interjected.

"I came to Montana to meet you, Rodney. You're my birth father, and yes, before you ask me, I'm sure. I'd love for it not to be true, but it is. My mom was a party girl, a buckle bunny, and I'm your daughter and—" she faltered "—you've never given me anything."

She paused and Jackson waited for Rodney to jump in and defend himself. But he didn't. Instead he looked at her, mouth slack-jawed and eyes wide.

"I guess what I want to know is, even though you've never given me anything, are you really going to make it your life's mission to take what little I have away? Is that the kind of man you are?"

Jackson watched her, his chest filling with pride. Everything Hannah had, she'd earned. Every fight, she'd survived. And she'd risked it all for him. It was the most empowering realization he'd ever had. Hannah Bean loved him.

He kept eye contact with Rodney just long enough to see Rodney's head shake from side to side. "I'm not going to go against my own kin. I already told Jackson, I'm—"

Hannah held her hand up. "This is my fault too. You didn't know it was me. I didn't give you the chance to be your best self, I know that now. But after all this, I just don't know what I'm ready for."

She turned and walked away from the table. Jackson pulled a fifty from his money clip, placing it in front of Rodney. "Keep all the money from the Cardic deal. All of it. And make sure to become the kind of guy that's worthy of her."

As Jackson ran out, he heard Rodney shout behind him, "You, too, Jackson. You be worthy of her too."

That was one piece of advice he'd take.

"Hannah!"

She heard him coming after her and quickened her pace. She didn't want Jackson to see her like this. Cheeks wet with tears. Face hot with shame.

"Hannah," Jackson called again, this time closer. She heard the clip of his boots quickening behind her. At once, the hospital seemed all too big and all too small at the same time.

She felt his hand on her arm, urging her to stop, urging her to turn.

She did, spearing him with her sharp eyes. "Tricking me into lunch? Letting me get my hopes up? Haven't you had enough fun for today, Brad, Jackson, whoever you are today?" She glared at him. It was easier being angry than sad.

"Said the masseuse, doctor, expiration girlfriend, whoever you are today," he teased. Unlike her, his voice was light.

"Can't you just leave me alone?" She met his eyes with hers, finally unashamed by her tears.

He took another step, standing a little too close, and Hannah felt aware of him with every fiber in her body, with every iota of her soul. He was close enough for her to smell pine and bergamot and liniment seed oil. He was close enough for her to feel safe.

"I can't," he whispered.

"'Can't'?" she repeated incomprehensibly.

"I can't leave you alone. See, the thing is, I love you."

She stopped breathing. Stopped blinking. "What? You can't. Amelia…she said I broke you. And, Jackson? I can't stop thinking that you broke me right back." Her voice caught with the disclosure.

He lifted his hand to her face, letting the pad of his thumb trace against her cheekbone then fall to the curve of her jaw. With his other hand, he pushed the hair from her brow and tilted her chin.

"That's the problem with you city folk." He smiled. "You think breaking something wild is bad. Hell, what do I know? Maybe it is. But I think you're looking at it all wrong. Breaking horses, at least for me, was always about coming to an understanding with the animal. Coming to an understanding with the part of it that's wild. You don't break horses in any other sense, not if you're doing it right, and you sure as hell didn't break me. But, Hannah, my Hannah, I think, just maybe, you went one further. Maybe you *understand* me."

She was quiet and he continued.

"I'm done risking everything trying to prove a point that doesn't even matter. I used to think I needed to earn love. That I needed to be the best. Prove that I was enough."

"You are enough." Her hand flew to his chest, tracing the hard muscle with her small fingers.

"Now, I don't need to prove anything anymore. Because I love you. You make me feel enough. I don't need a buckle, I need a ring. I need you in my life, as my wife. I need to be with you always."

He was quiet for a moment and she felt that moment drag into eternity.

"Thing is, I'm not sure I'll have much time to rodeo now. I called Cardic Motors today, and they loved my idea." His thumb was back, stroking her cheek.

"You called Cardic?"

"Yeah, I told them about the mustangs on our section of Yellowstone. Proposed they change their marketing campaign from rodeo to wild. 'Cardic—the Generational Choice of the Wild West and Proud Supporter of the Hartmann Pryor Mustang Sanctuary.'" He grinned at her and she melted.

"There's a Pryor mustang sanctuary?" she managed to ask.

"There is now. Now that I'm here to run it, among other things. I'm staying, but I need more. I need to build my life with someone who understands me. Do you think you can do that?"

Both hands were back cupping her face, his honey eyes searching hers.

"No," she breathed. "I'll do you one better."

He smiled at her and it felt like the sun warming her soul.

"I'll love you. Forever."

Then Jackson Hartmann kissed her.

Finally, he had come home.

* * * * *

Look for Amelia's story, coming soon!

Only from Katie Frey and Harlequin Desire.

#2923 ONE NIGHT RANCHER

The Carsons of Lone Rock • by Maisey Yates

To buy the property, bar owner Cara Thompson must spend one night at a ghostly hotel and asks her best friend, Jace Carson, to join her. But when forbidden kisses melt into passion, *both* are haunted by their explosive encounter...

#2924 A COWBOY KIND OF THING

Texas Cattleman's Club: The Wedding • by Reese Ryan

Tripp Nobel is convinced Royal, Texas, is perfect for his famous cousin's wedding. But convincing Dionna Reed, the bride's Hollywood best friend...? The wealthy rancher's kisses soon melt her icy shell, but will they be enough to tempt her to take on this cowboy?

#2925 RODEO REBEL

Kingsland Ranch • by Joanne Rock

With a successful bull rider in her bachelor auction, Lauryn Hamilton's horse rescue is sure to benefit. But rodeo star Gavin Kingsley has his devilish, bad boy gaze on *her*. The good girl. The one who's never ruled by reckless passion—until now...

#2926 THE INHERITANCE TEST

by Anne Marsh

Movie star Declan Masterson needs to rehabilitate his playboy image fast to save his inheritance! Partnering with Jane Charlotte—the quintessential "plain jane"—for a charity yacht race is a genius first step. If only there wasn't a captivating woman underneath Jane's straightlaced exterior...

#2927 BILLIONAIRE FAKE OUT

The Image Project • by Katherine Garbera

Paisley Campbell just learned her lover is a famous Hollywood A-lister... and she's expecting his baby! Sean O'Neill knows he's been living on borrowed time by keeping his identity secret. Can he convince her that everything they shared was not just a celebrity stunt?

#2928 A GAME OF SECRETS

The Eddington Heirs • by Zuri Day

CEO Jake Eddington was charged with protecting his friend's beautiful sister from players and users. And he knows *he* should resist their chemistry too...but socialite Sasha McDowell is too captivating to ignore—even if their tryst ignites a scandal...

HDCNM1222

Get 4 FREE REWARDS!

We'll send you 2 FREE Books plus 2 FREE Mystery Gifts.

FREE Value Over $20

Both the **Harlequin® Desire** and **Harlequin Presents®** series feature compelling novels filled with passion, sensuality and intriguing scandals.

YES! Please send me 2 FREE novels from the Harlequin Desire or Harlequin Presents series and my 2 FREE gifts (gifts are worth about $10 retail). After receiving them, if I don't wish to receive any more books, I can return the shipping statement marked "cancel." If I don't cancel, I will receive 6 brand-new Harlequin Presents Larger-Print books every month and be billed just $6.30 each in the U.S. or $6.49 each in Canada, a savings of at least 10% off the cover price, or 6 Harlequin Desire books every month and be billed just $5.05 each in the U.S. or $5.74 each in Canada, a savings of at least 12% off the cover price. It's quite a bargain! Shipping and handling is just 50¢ per book in the U.S. and $1.25 per book in Canada.* I understand that accepting the 2 free books and gifts places me under no obligation to buy anything. I can always return a shipment and cancel at any time by calling the number below. The free books and gifts are mine to keep no matter what I decide.

Choose one: ☐ **Harlequin Desire**
(225/326 HDN GRJ7)

☐ **Harlequin Presents Larger-Print**
(176/376 HDN GRJ7)

Name (please print)

Address   Apt. #

City   State/Province   Zip/Postal Code

Email: Please check this box ☐ if you would like to receive newsletters and promotional emails from Harlequin Enterprises ULC and its affiliates. You can unsubscribe anytime.

Mail to the **Harlequin Reader Service:**
IN U.S.A.: P.O. Box 1341, Buffalo, NY 14240-8531
IN CANADA: P.O. Box 603, Fort Erie, Ontario L2A 5X3

Want to try 2 free books from another series? Call 1-800-873-8635 or visit www.ReaderService.com.

HARLEQUIN
PLUS

Announcing a **BRAND-NEW**
multimedia subscription service
for romance fans like you!

Read, Watch and Play.

Experience the easiest way to get
the romance content you crave.

Start your **FREE 7 DAY TRIAL** at
<u>www.harlequinplus.com/freetrial</u>.